DIRTY PEACE

Nathan Nakonieczny

PAGE PUBLISHING, INC.
Conneaut Lake, PA

First originally published by Page Publishing 2020

ISBN 978-1-64701-298-4 (pbk)
ISBN 978-1-64701-299-1 (digital)

Printed in the United States of America

For my mother, on her iron shoes, with all her trusty bags.

The sweet aroma of life floats about my limbs,
Though I could sink down if danger was on the wind,
But for now I keep my trunk high,
And gaze upon the bliss going by.
Two lovers, sweet youth enthralls them,
The hint of privacy guiding their whim,
And they dare a humble kiss.
But who will kiss the tree?
When the aether sends fire,
Or the floods bring about a mire,
Who will bend to kiss the tree?
Several pups, rushing and dancing and chattering about,
One said play ball, another said tag,
One of the lads is encaped, playing a hag.
What sweet youth. When I were young and my roots were small,
I believed that I was so tall.
These children see how they were,
And see how they are,
And think themselves big even though their life will stretch far.
They do not know, of how their limbs they will grow,
And the leaf shedding,
And the frights of snow,
And the lonely nights of woe,
And the ache and lust to simply go.

Who will listen to the tree?
Is it the saws for which I am summoned?
Is it my stump, ripped from its earthy womb?
Is it the wind that blows strong since I have no body now to command?
Is it this noisy mill which my trunk calls its tomb?
No. No one will listen to the tree.

OH, LONG NIGHT STORM

An empty couch, I'm on the ground. My rat is pecking against his plastic tub. I remember when I got that little fella. Found him in my basement. No other cage than a plastic tub I cut holes in. My roomie said he's a freaky pest and to get rid of him. I think he's all right. He loves me, I'm sure, just bites sometimes.

I can't remember the last time I got up. It's been seven-bowls-and-an-entire-box of crayons kind of night. I can't remember what I did with the crayons. Standing up is certainly more tiring than I had imagined, and I immediately fell back down. My shitty eighties orange ceiling makes me uncomfortable. I'll remember to burn it as soon as possible.

Crouching for the rest of my life seems like a good idea. I'll find myself a little box and put it over me, draw a little shell on the outside. It'll be beautiful. I think my roomie just got home. I got to find a box as soon as possible. I hear his feet and someone else's.

My crouch-flustering didn't help me find a box, so I just lifted up the couch and turned it over me. Diablo watches judgingly from the corner of the room, thinking how much he wants an overturned couch. Lame.

"Luke, what In the name of national socialism are you doing!" I've been caught.

"Who's the babe?" I barely peered up from my half-triangle fort.

"This beautiful *lady* Carmen is going to be staying here with us for a while."

The hem of her dress was ugly as hell. It was a weird green doily pattern, split down the middle to show off half her legs. Ugly ass dress.

"How much did you pick her up for?"

"Fuck off, Luke!" Oh, she knows my name now. Fabulous. Wait, I know her voice from somewhere. Whatever, not interested.

"Hey, Michael, grab Diablo for me."

He left me with a "No fucking way, pal" and barged up the stairs. This gave me two options. (1) Wait until they inevitably bang and go fuck with them. Not in the way you're thinking, more like super glue his shorts to the ceiling and wait until he notices. (2) Leave, because that's weird, and I know he would probably decapitate me, or Carmen would. I need some Oreos anyway.

So the first trial was exiting the couch fort. I decided it was best to leave it overturned, considering Michael was an asshole. I also opted out of leaving my bong on the floor. I had to commit an Indiana Jones-style heist, measuring the weight of the bong, estimating the weight of Diablo. With a quick flick of the wrist, Diablo was squeaking in my hand, and my bong was safely hidden in a plastic tub. Insert wrecking ball.

My jacket was upstairs in my room, sketchy two-bedroom house in the industrial area. Trains really got to me; we lived not even three blocks from a railway. Big freight trains came by every day. My whole area smelled of soot, pitch, and dead children. Trains always hit children, doncha know, the rural ones. All those dirty kids being raised by racist drunks, they don't want to be like their parents, so they jump in front of trains. I don't know if that's what happens, but the way these trains looked, I wouldn't doubt it. Anyway, I don't much like locomotives.

There wasn't any sign they were at it yet, so I tried to be real quiet. Wouldn't want a fancy working gal like her to get spooked by another creepy twenty-three-year-old man in the house. Didn't see any part of her but her weird feet. She had on these big high heels that went about three inches up. You could tell the dress was too long for her because it hung just halfway up the heel, without heels she'd be walking on it. I guess that's kinda cute, though, someone wearing a dress too long for them and just compensating for it. She probably didn't get enough business to get her dress fixed.

Walking into my room was dreadful, can't remember ever having anyone in here. I remember some gal came in here when Michael had a little shindig with all his friends. I could tell that she was the least picky of her group, because she settled on talking with me all night. Sat in there, got to freaking mars, and then sold her car online together. It was intimate as all hell, talking about the suitable prices, nearly kissed while looking up older models. I don't know her name, but I know she doesn't have a Subaru anymore.

My jacket was old too. It had holes in the elbows for how little I lift my arms. I was still riding a pretty good afterglow, so I decided to hunt down my sketchbook. Maybe I'd draw the Oreos. On my way down the stairs, I discovered where my crayons had gone. In my bathroom, I had a bowl of rainbow swirled wax and a spoon sitting on the sink. I had melted my crayons down and tried to eat them. It was not my proudest moment.

As I was collecting my aged, beaten-up shoes, I was realizing how little I'd done in the past many hours. I had no clue what time it was, no idea where I was going. I *could have* caused World War III and I wouldn't know it until I left. Diablo was currently eating some of the wax I'd pulled out of the bowl. I'm sure he loved it. Purple and orange are his favorite flavors.

So I set off into the night. My small limbs shook in response to the chilly air, but Oreos called to me. I knew the next Plaid Pantry was about a mile down the bridge, but it was a journey worth taking. The trains didn't run at… darkness time? Whatever time it was, there would be no trains. I boycott them very firmly. I kinda balanced on the concrete bumper, even though I could've walked on the sidewalk. I was surprised I could balance really.

There weren't too many houses before it became industrial. Like you'd have a nice pretty suburban house and then an oil refinery next door. Not the prettiest place in Washington. There used to be this goth babe that lived next door. I think she jumped off the bridge, though. I guess this is as good a place as any to live your last. Sucks, though, she was pretty nice.

Diablo decided now was an appropriate time to begin biting my shoulder, so I let him. Rats can't have much joy in life, so biting shoulders is the least they can do. I probably got rabies several times. Just such a crazy freak I never noticed it. Made me think how Carmen would react to having her shoulders bitten. She'd probably scream or something.

The bridge past the refinery is huge. It goes over the Columbia into Oregon, and I guess there's a Plaid Pantry on the other side. There were only a few cars on it at this time of night, or maybe I was dead and I was in limbo and that was why there were no cars. Who the hell knows these days?

There were always people sitting and begging on this bridge. I saw one guy just a few hundred feet down, didn't even have a sign. As I was walking up to him, I saw he got a really long beard, and he was flicking a quarter in the air.

"Hey, man, why you out at this time of night? Like the lights?" He looked up as I was about to pass, so I had to talk to him.

"Nah, just nowhere to stay, kid. Why are you out?"

"Roomie is being an alpha male again, can't handle it."

He looked puzzled. "I don't got a clue what that means." If that didn't state his confusion, he continued having that "I'm homeless and uneducated and I don't know what you just said" kind of look. A lot of them pretended to be dumber than they are, thinking people would pity them more.

"It means he brought some prostitute home and I don't want anything to do with it."

He kind of cough-sighed and flipped his coin again before responding. "Yeah, I had a pal like that once, always picking up girls and showing off."

"So what happened to him?"

"I stabbed him seventeen times."

"Yeah, I feel ya, I really want to stab Michael sometimes."

"The issue is they usually die when you do. Or at least get pretty pissed off."

This man was a prophet. "Yeah, I understand completely. I might go get some Oreos, want me to bring you a package on my way back around?"

"Well, sure, son, you got a toke?"

My man. "Absolutely, I'll getcha on the way back around."

I don't know what it was, but that man seemed like he should have had a dog. A dog would have been very appropriate, give him a reason to live or something.

The rest of the bridge was uneventful, a few pairs of shoes and some sleeping bags. Bums leave them here to come back to. No one has the heart to take them, or the desire to. These sights were very pretty, looking over this huge river and seeing all the city lights. I decided it would have been a good idea to be nice to that Carmen gal. Maybe she would've favored me if I was nice enough.

This bridge had a way of making you remember things you didn't want to remember. Not just that, it had been thirty-five minutes and my afterglow was dying. It looked like it was going to rain. Back in high school when it rained, there was this gal I used to hang around who hated it. Same kinda gal as that Carmen chick, wore high heels even in the rain. She had a height inferiority complex even though she was plenty tall. She was as tall as she needed to be but kept making herself seem taller. Standing straight up and puffing out her chest to make her look real tall. It was funny. She always acted very mature too, as if you didn't know she had an inferiority complex. Then it began to rain.

I ended up getting off the bridge before it began raining. The wind started pelting me with rain as soon as I hit sidewalk, though. Diablo was hiding in my pocket. Diablo wasn't even a real pet rat, just a rat I found and decided to keep. No wonder he was so temperamental. He was wild. The Plaid was just a few blocks away, I thought. The thing about Portland is, it's not at all safe at night. Not because people are out to get you, just because there's no people where people should be and vice versa.

Heroin needles and hobos slept on the streets I walked, but from a corner, I could see my holy grail, shining with its yellow-golden sign piercing the shadows. Plaid Pantry shown above all else on this dreary cold night.

The place is an interesting hostel. It just looks like it should fill up space. Never looks in fashion anywhere. The white bricks don't match any others; the blue and red paint don't help none. It's open twenty-four hours, though, so my quest was fulfilled.

The store greeted me with the scent of long-emptied grease and stale hair extensions. The woman at the counter looked incredibly bored and very spacey, which she probably was. It was dark a.m., and she had work. The potato chips and Doritos watched my rushed hunting. There were no Oreos in the cookie section, none in the hostess section, none in any section they should have been. Surely I could have settled for Chips Ahoy or Keebler, but it was the principle of it. The symbol of going somewhere to get something, and I was damn well going to buy it.

"Excuse me, miss, there's no Oreos."

"Oh."

Ex-fucking-scuse me. "There's none in the aisle they belong in."

"It's four thirty-five in the morning, we don't restock until seven."

I walked up to her and looked her dead in the eye. She had a pair of those fake contact lenses that make your eyes look purple, and in any other circumstance I would think it's dank as hell. Not now, though. This was war.

"Now I know for a fact that you have Oreos in the stockroom. You keep extra stock of everything in case a truck doesn't show up at 7:00 a.m. like it's supposed to. I know you probably bought those lenses from Etsy, and they look beautiful on you, but that doesn't mean you're not withholding Oreos from me."

Fuck.

"Listen, sir, thank you for the compliment, but I have no interest in breaking the rules of my establishment. I really need the money."

"All right, well then, take a break and pilfer them."

"I can't just do that."

"This is the United States of America."

"Land of the enslaved."

"Cute. I'm waiting till seven."

"Fine by me."

She continued looking bored. She was an all right-looking gal, kinda big, huge caverns in her ears, dark-blue hair. She looked like a cliché punk rocker combined with new age hipster. Sweet lord. Then I saw she had some goddamn Oreos in her purse. Sitting a few feet from her on a stool and inaccessible to me. They were a small pack of maybe six to eight Oreos, one of them cheap two-dollar packages.

I tried to look at her again, but she was checking her phone. It was the kind of look on her face from someone who clearly hates your presence. My mind thought of every movie I'd ever seen where the annoying guy ends up falling in love with the bitchy side actress. I thought of being that annoying guy. Maybe I'm really the sad guy that ends up jumping off the bridge a few blocks away after being rejected by a woman in a Plaid Pantry. Maybe I'm that desperate that the first human contact besides Michael in two weeks has been a crazy hobo and a punk chick in a Plaid Pantry. All this I thought while staring at her kickass contact lenses.

The air outside was welcoming. It was cold as hell, reminded me of a winter several years ago. Reminded me of Carmen again. I only knew one Carmen in my lifetime. That was that girl I knew in high school. The one that tried to act all tough and prideful and classy. I talked to her once, or a lot; I can't really remember. She was in my friend group kinda. I hung out with the stoners, all of 'em eventually getting lives and moving on. Carmen thought I was funny. She thought I was a great friend and loved how I was always there to talk to her and make her feel good.

"Luke, why are you always so down?" she said to me on a rainy day like tonight.

"What do you mean, kiddo?"

"Stop, Luke, you're only two years older than me, okay!" She always had this singsong voice. It was so pretty. I always told her she could be a singer, but she never believed me.

"You're still a kiddo. You'll always be my kiddo." I talked so happy back then. I talked with passion.

"Luke! You know what I meant though! If you're not complimenting me or reminding me how important I am, you're being down on yourself. You're a very talented man, Luke." She moved her face close to mine then. I smelled like pot all the time, while she smelled like all the oceans spraying down on me.

"Carmen…just promise you'll never forget me when you go off."

"I'll be back in half a decade, Luke! I know it's not too long, I just really want to be a teacher. You know, like that one that made us sit next to each other! He was such a nice guy freshman year. I wanna be like that."

I loved when she talked like that. I loved when she talked. I just wish we could talk like that more often. She was so bright, graduated sophomore year.

"I loved old Mr. Spicer! He was a great guy. I'm glad he inspired you. I'm happy for you." I wasn't being serious. I didn't want her to go. I wish she could just stay, and I'd watch the rest of her existence forever. I would watch her from beginning to end. She was my favorite movie, my favorite person, my only love.

Flash-forward. Same freezing cold raining night. Only four years ago. A thousand Skype calls, a thousand "Not now, Luke's, a thousand tears, a million thoughts of her, a trillion thoughts about life and only one person I cared about. But her…

A hundred boyfriends, a thousand "Luke, we were never in love"s, a thousand seconds of self-awareness, a thousand pills that couldn't kill me, a thousand "Fuck, why am I even alive"s. And only one person. Ten calls she answered, ten boyfriends she asked my advice about. I could spend all fucking night thinking about how I was hurt, if a purple-lensed angel didn't pass me a cigarette.

"Listen, it's been a long night for everyone. I know you aren't angry about the Oreos. That was real nice, normal people tell me my lenses look dumb. I picked 'em when I was back in high school, thought they looked cool and edgy. They're actually just regular contacts." She lit my smoke, which to my surprise she didn't have one. "I figured I'd piece one with you."

"Yeah, thanks. I think they really are great. Boyfriend is a lucky guy."

"Girlfriend."

"Fuck."

"I know, I had brothers that bitched about it all the time."

"You're just the first girl to talk to me without saying 'fuck' offensively."

"I can say 'fuck' in-offensively."

"This is a Plaid Pantry, you're at work, and I'm very sad. No, thank you."

"Was worth a shot."

"That's not the point. I'm just getting tired of slutty women."

"Why? We're perfectly fine. Guys are no different."

"Not me, I fucking hate 'em. Sluts of any gender freak me out. I live with one, and now apparently two. My roommate brought a working girl home that looks and sounds like my ex, who I'm pretending doesn't exist because she fucked me up."

"Kill yourself?"

"Thought about it, water ain't my best friend."

"I was joking 'cause you said you hate me. But seriously, bro, that's no fun." She got sad all of a sudden. Not that it had been all rainbows to begin with, but I certainly didn't mean to ruin her morning.

I sighed. "What's your name anyway? Might as well vent to someone I know."

"Carmen, what's yours?"

"Fuck you, what's your real name?"

"Carmen!" That was a trip.

"That's the name of my ex and Michael's new girl."

"Well, maybe you're tripping on your carpet at home and fabricated my entire existence. Either way, I'm gonna give you a package of Oreos. See ya, Luke."

So she did, getting up quickly and tossing it to me. How did she know my name? She said 'Dude' probably, and I just heard it weird because I hadn't slept in god knows how long. It was six or so. The bus was running.

Even though the bus was running, I felt like walking a mile back home. Spilling my guts to a Plaid Pantry Bisexual wasn't my morning's intentions. It made me think maybe that was my Carmen, the one that's been gone. I knew she wouldn't want anything to do with me. Michael was a great alpha. At least I had a disgusting rat to bite me for all eternity.

That homeless man wasn't there when I came back. I'm guessing he left or jumped off. Maybe both. Who knows. It makes you wonder how the world looks to normal people. What they think when they see a homeless guy that admitted to stabbing his friend to death. Do they respond positively?

The rest of my walk was filled with thoughts about eating glass and other entertaining things. I couldn't really think positively. My voyage had taken such a lame turn, and I was coming down. I was coming down. It's a terrible feeling when you get sad by the end of the end of your high, and you know it'll fuck up your whole day. At least for me.

Michael was on the patio smoking a cigarette, shirtless and sculpted as always. I had Diablo in my hand, currently eating a good portion of my thumb, which I should get checked out at a later date. Michael was a little startled, with my hand bleeding and everything, and he said he'd get a towel.

"Nah, dude, it matches the pain in my soul," I said, sitting on the third step and looking down at the rat.

"A-all right, man. Where'd you go, dude? Are you on a downer man?" He looked worried though I knew he wasn't. He was just playing, trying to look good for Mrs. Ugly Dress.

"Chill. The only downer I've taken is life."

"This is a problem. Put the rat in the box, and we're going to talk about this."

"All right, I'm realizing I probably do need the rest of my thumb."

It hadn't occurred to me that this rat was actually eating my thumb and that he was probably very dangerous, considering I would have to later cauterize this. So rather than putting him in the box, I threw him back into the basement from whence he came.

Flick, burner, wait two minutes, hold towel to hand, don't get blood all over the kitchen, feel pain, hate myself, place thumb on burner, scream in pain. Wait for Michael to run inside, hear him scream what am I doing, tell me to take my hand off the burner, put the rest of my hand on the burner, second-degree burns.

By this point adrenaline had killed my sorrow completely. I didn't have any thought process going on. I'd only roomed with Michael for a year, so he'd never seen this part of me.

I suppose this kind of thing was normal for me. Two years ago I had one of these episodes. I had a breakdown or something. Fucked up my fists getting into a fight with this guy. Was my twenty-first birthday, found a pretty lady, got really intoxicated, started talking to her like I did Carmen. She got creeped out, some guy stepped in, and I beat him to near death. It's not a happy memory. I tried to forget everything that happened in my life before that. I didn't really feel like talking about it, but I guess this was the peak.

I sat in my basement for another twenty-five minutes, waiting for the jitters to fly away. My hand swelled a lot, definitely would have to lop it off as soon as possible. Reality kinda came back to me there, so I walked up the stairs.

"Michael, where is Carmen?"

"What…why the fuck would you want to talk to her? I never heard about any of this shit you're dealing with, I don't really want to—"

"Not what I asked. Where is Carmen?"

"Uh, upstairs, man. Can you please explain this to me later? I've never seen you this angry before."

I didn't really bother talking to him. My jeans were soaked, and I hadn't showered since last night. If this was my ex, then I guess this'd be the best way to meet her. I knocked, why the hell did I knock? She didn't answer, so I pushed the door in.

She wasn't how I remembered her. She wasn't as tan. Not as chubby as she was. She looked like someone took my ol' Carmen and stretched her out but then pushed her back down again. She wasn't in that weird green dress anymore, but she was in a green blanket on Michael's bed.

"Hey. How was college?" I tried to be casual, sitting down on the bed next to her feet.

"Micha—Luke? I thought you left last night...or something. Hi, how have you been? Can you give me a bit to g—What happened to your hand?"

"I don't know, not important. Why are you on Michael's bed?"

"Because he let me stay here...He thought you'd be happy to see me and let me sleep up there and..." She sighed, trying to sit up. She tried to keep herself covered, though, showing me she clearly wasn't clothed. "Listen, I was stressed after a long flight...you know how I am, and well, Michael was there."

I guess that was what I was waiting for. I was waiting for some confirmation that, yes, she did sleep with him, and yes, that was my ex-girlfriend. "No. I don't know how you are, you never used to be that way. You haven't talked to me for years, so I didn't know you were a fucking nymphomaniac."

She kinda half gasped, but not dramatic like in the movies. An actual gasp. "Luke...I figured you knew that...listen, it's really early and—"

"Knew that what."

"Knew that I'd been cheating on you...I'm just not really happy with one guy. I thought you listened to the rumors, that you figured when we..." She paused.

This was a crossroads. I could always go with the "Washington man murders roommate and ex-girlfriend then jumps off the Glenn Jackson bridge" path, or I could begin crying. I decided to go with neither and kissed her. This wasn't the kind of movie kiss. This was the kind where my mouth was dry and hers tasted like my roommate's semen. Our tongues didn't know what to do. It was so forced from both parties that I think we both silently gagged at the end of it.

This was the girl that had ruined my life for five years. Funny thing about love is, even if it's not mutual, you can't help wanting the other person to feel happy. I hated her more than anything in that second, but I still loved her. So I handed her her dress and left the room for her to come out. After I heard a half-ass chipper "I'm ready," I entered again.

It was kinda like a second chance when I opened it again. She stood there, in that ugly frilled dress without high heels, smiling with her hands at her sides. I kinda got used to her new pale skinniness in a second. It was a different her. So I hugged her. At first she cringed, unexpecting and didn't want to, but then she hugged back. I was still way taller than her, so her head was pressed against my chest. Her breathing was rougher than it was, more gruff.

"You smoke now?"

"Yeah. Had nothing better to do for a year. I dropped out in senior year."

"Figured. You know I hate you more than anything, right? I actually just flipped a coin in my head on whether I would cry or murder you. It landed on the edge of the coin."

"Yeah, I know. That's how it's always been with you. Figured you wouldn't change."

"You were right. Fuckin' bitch."

For some reason she hugged me tighter then. It was like she felt my anger and knew I wouldn't stay angry. She knew I would forgive her a few hours later. I'd still distrust her, but we'd be "all right." That was how this shit always was.

"You really hung on…I'm so sorry. Just because I didn't love you then, I thought you didn't love me. I guess I came to apologize. Guess what though?" I kinda sighed in response to that.

"No, guess." She prodded.

"What?"

"I still don't," she whispered this in my ear so sensually I could have sworn it was a sweet nothing. She always did that, say something real rude in a sweet tone. "Though I can."

"Not interested."

"Are you kidding me? I flew all the way over here, prepared some shitty speech on how even though I don't love you, I'm willing to try again because you spent five years waiting and all that shit."

"Not interested."

She kissed my cheek, my other cheek, my neck. I figured she'd be crying, which she was doing right now. I wanted nothing more than to be dead right this moment. The whole universe rearranges itself in a night, and here I was, every atom in my body being attracted to every molecule in her body. By the time we were able to conceptualize we were dead, our carbon would have already been stolen by something out there. The universe split us into this position in time-space, and here I was, fucking it up.

I sat down on the bed, and she wrapped herself over me, her chin on my shoulders. We just sat like that, no words, no emotion, just existence. Then she moved her head closer to my ear, her tongue flicking against it, and she whispered, "The chemical that creates dreams, dimethyltryptamine, is released at an extensive rate when we die. You could be hallucinating your entire life in the last six to thirty minutes of it. Why not make the best of it?"

SELLING YOUR SOUL

There are no crickets in the city. I have waited up every night sitting at this fancy desk, waiting for a chirp or a whistle or a croak or something to tell me I'm alive. "The money's good," everyone tells me, but I fear I'm going to go insane. If this persists any longer, I'm afraid I'll allow it, as long as it promises me bliss. Content. No location you visit in an occupation like mine, like this. This is just surviving, and I don't believe I can make it to the next quota whilst suffering the weight of these longer-than-afternoon nights.

All I do is work until I'm exhausted and then try to sleep as best I can. It oddly reminds me of my childhood. Wandering around late, always assuming when I'm an adult I won't get to do that ever again. I was half right. If there ever was such a thing.

Crows are abundant, though. Almost as if they eat the flesh of all the rotting souls in this city. Not that that is possible, but surely they like the dark atmosphere. The gloom calms them, makes them squawk and shriek. The darkness is how a crow lives; it's the happiness and sadness. Perhaps it's the smog that is ever overhanging. I wish there was some way for me to not end up like a crow, but from the length of my stay here, the feathers should be coming in shortly.

I fear the worst. I feel the gloom, once produced by the brick-and-picket inhabitants, is something I must carry and that may, any day now, smother what life is left, like hopeless flame. I kick back the last of my glass and turn the corner, which leads me through the kitchen and den to my quarters. I've always despised this layout. It seems as one would imagine a charnel house would be, rows of cramped apartments, room enough for a bed and your few earthly possessions. And the box.

I can feel the insomnia in the air. No one, in any of these rooms, has slipped from their consciousness. I won't be sleeping. I will merely close my eyes and pretend I'm not here. When they open, it will be another day. There is no real sleep, no real rest. What rest can I have when all I have to look forward to is the same thing. It feels like I'm the only one who realizes it, one small voice in countless legions of corporate zombies. I need to do something. On my bedside table.

Today I rise as I always do. I sit and listen to traffic and make the best attempts I can to barricade the annoyance by focusing on the drip, drip, drop from the percolator on the opposite counter. After less than fruitful trials, I set out in the usual fashion. Down four blocks, left turn followed by a right followed by another left turn. It is the same. My desk, decorated with books I've never read and pictures of families that ain't mine. "It makes you look friendly, whether you act it or not." I hear the words as if they were leaving Henry's girth, as if it were this very day. One hundred and sixty-seven days. That's how long it's been since I'd talked with him. Henry was not the best of sights, nor the best in communication, but he was the only other original person in this damned city. I wasn't original then. I'm not original now, but I still remember that he made me feel like I was. I can't remember our conversation, something about cars or women or something terrible like that. I can't bother with him anymore, though he was the only thing worth a bother. But that time, his time here, has passed, and now I am left with the remembrance of occasions where I could have potentially convinced him to stay.

Feet keep shuffling by me, past me, and through me. I know they're there, but I can't look up. *Tip tap*, due dates race. *Tap tip*, the word quota burns into me like hot coals. *Tip tap tip*, tasks for the day complete after a short trip to the eighth floor followed by another tip tap task to add to the list. There used to be a Ferris wheel near here. I can't remember where it was. I never ended up going. At least I knew it was there. At least.

Maybe next week will be the week my plans go through, but not today or any day before Friday, the day my work is reviewed, but maybe next week, I will do it. Drowsiness has finally hit. Maybe in the spring. I could get used to this. Maybe. I'm not sure what the higher-ups will be reviewing, but people leave around those times. I can't even remember what it is I do, day in, day out. I've been doing it so long it's natural, the typing and stamping and calling and managing. Never have to think anymore, though.

Another cup of coffee. It's night again. Most people have left. Hopefully one day they'll all leave and I can sit at my desk without being bothered by another human being. I don't dislike people; it's just been so long since I've met one that has anything interesting to say. It kind of reminds me of when I saw a rabbit, long ago. I don't like them now. It was a small little rabbit. It looked sad, all white and soft and, for some reason, so lost. It seemed to like me, but I figured it would be much happier with other rabbits. I brought it to an animal sanctuary to help integrate it into nature. I didn't know that rabbits could be outcasts, and the extremes a whole species would go through to exile one member. It's sad, humans think they're so different than animals, but a leg out of place is a leg lost. A rabbit out of place is one killed by the pack.

I've begun thinking again. I need to make a mental note not to do that. Henry always told me when I was overthinking something. Always said that though I didn't know it, I was a free thinker. I wish he had been honest with me, told me I was only a free thinker when he wanted me to be, and any other time was out of his understanding. The dent I left in his wall is still there, so many days later. The couch hasn't been replaced. I don't have to see these things. I just know him and know he wouldn't change anything.

The rain outside pelts the windows. I think everyone has gone home now. I take a moment to walk along the painted plywood and cheap metal cubicles. Some people have photos, knickknacks. One person has a beta fish. It's fun, seeing pieces of life. I'm sure they are only pieces. There is no one out there that could manage a whole life and work. It's just not that kind of job. It's a kind of job that you stay up to live through.

23

There's a face somewhere in this room attached to a piece of glass. It's unfamiliar. It's been so long since I looked in a mirror. Unworthy, unshaven, shabby, big-nosed, uncomfortable, disgusting, pockmarked, unruly. My face was something I always worried about. It reminded me of Henry. A time, not long ago, standing in a place where I was looking at a mirror. I never liked my face. It's boring and unnatural. Everything about it is wrong. The night had been long, the drinking had been much, and the sounds were animalistic. The party was something I didn't want a part of. Henry was shuffling about, bare torso, prideful, and war hungry. His aimless wandering led him to me.

"Hey, you having a good time?"

"I'm trying to get ready."

"You've been getting ready for three hours." His smile is so darling and earnest.

"I don't feel at place."

"I'm right here with you, you don't need to be ashamed of anything." His smile is a triple barbed hook.

Another lie. Another night. His stinking breath against my shoulder, in that cramped restroom we shared, that room we shared with hundreds of people, sharing the same fetid air. It's terrible. I always hated parties. I only bothered going because he invited me. It was our house, but he invited me. I was holding the box, all shiny and new.

Another staple, another spreadsheet passing through a mailbox to someone I'll never meet. The birds are clustering on the high peaks out my window. They want to take me. They know I've been lost a long time. Another nail slammed into my coffin. The beating of shoes on this carpeted ground reminds me of coupling. It's uncomfortable.

Many bodies all attached. It began around four thirty. I'd been down with Henry for a few hours. He forced me to have…fun. It wasn't fun. I didn't know any of these people. Apparently they went to his high school. He drank more, becoming less sentient as it went. I tried to stop him, but he assumed it was helping him. I suppose it did. It helped him land into a woman's lap and helped get rid of me until the next morning. I wasn't sure what I was supposed to do when he'd left. A woman tried talking with me; I showed no interest.

She tried all night. I didn't notice her. She'd seen my anxiety in the restroom. Thought I was lonely, kept waiting for me to move. She told me all this. I felt bad, how her imagination could turn a boring meaningless person into her Prince Charming. I told her nothing. I said nothing more than was necessary. She kept drinking. Henry kept fucking his whore. I kept sitting patiently. I was pulled. She thought I was playing hard to get. I was dragged into Henry's bedroom, the bodies stuck together, terrifying me. My shirt was thrown, and then my hand was thrown. The room was colder. None had seen my act as more than rough foreplay. The only one who noticed me leave and saw the girl cry was Henry. In that moment, he worried for me. In that moment, I hated him.

The emptying of the coffeepot is always a saddening time. A sign that I have to make more, waste more money to keep making money. I've never held any of it, but it's all on plastic, so why does it matter? Luxuries fly in from countries that fit in my pocket. I am the corporation, just thousands of mes, clicking buttons and printing money. I slowly forget I'm a human, and I become a machine. I prefer being a machine.

I never knew why I had no appeal for women. It was strange. Queer man on the corporate ladder, can't let anyone know. A thousand laughs and rocks would be thrown at me for attempting to be like everyone else. I know there's no reason for me to work this dead-end job, but it makes good money, and it gives me something to waste my life on.

I have no memory of high school. I blocked it out. It wasn't fun in the least. No friends. "He looks at me strangely," they say. No chance at dances. No advice to give. No one to show emotion to. I never got bullied. I just got avoided. It was worse than bullying because at least when you're bullied, people feel sorry for you. No one feels sorry for the kid that doesn't talk, the kid that looked and wanted to be like everyone else but couldn't be, because he just dodged everyone.

I went to college, did the same thing there. I took economics because it was the only major that involved ruining people's lives without speaking to them. I don't mean to say my life was cynical, but it has been up until now. Up until this night, where I forget to work and type and all that bullshit.

I keep thinking, one of these days, I'll jump. Very easy access to tall buildings, very little motivation to live life. What life am I living?

I'm laughing. I don't know how long I've been laughing for. I don't know what time it is. I've been living a fucking joke! It's comedic, a man with so much potential wastes it because he wasn't ever noticed. He pawns off his life as unoriginal and falls in love with the only guy to ever notice him. Not even a story worth telling because it's one everyone's heard. I guess that's the joke. The joke is that I wasted it. It's the reason you laugh at a car accident on TV. It's so horrendous you see the comparison to yourself and love it. We all love knowing there's someone below us.

I suppose that's why I jumped. Why I decided it was time for me to go. Why I opened that window on that night, laughing hysterically and falling twenty-five stories down. I'd been driven to madness, and I never lived in anything else. I jumped, and I realized…I was already gone. I'd been gone years before. When your life flashes before your eyes and you have nothing to see, that's what I got. That's why I'm still here. It's all I ever knew. The box was in my pocket when I clocked in today, how strange.

THE BOY WHO PAINTED
THE UNIVERSE

A dark alley in northeast Portland. Four police cars all parked around. Two men in handcuffs sulking in different cars. An ambulance siren blares from far down the street. People flow in and out of a nearby McDonald's, and the corpse lies untouched, except for the three bullet holes covering his body. His long gray beard covered in blood, grubby shoes, spray paint can in hand. Open-shut case, homeless man tags a nearby wall. Gang members don't want him on their turf. Gets blown down.

"Tell me, Miss…Fehrfinch, what was your relation to the victim?" A question launched from a pompous officer in a pinstripe suit. His words echoed around the dark padded room, hitting the single metal table and the young lady who didn't belong.

"My relation? On paper, none." Her dress was tight-fitting, tailored to her. Her hair well groomed. Her makeup was almost all green. This was her only opportunity to be in questioning. Her life was simply too fantastic.

"Then why, may I ask, were you found at the scene of the crime, doing nothing? You didn't call the police when he was committing vandalism or when he was being murdered. Is this a sick little game to you? Did you set it up for that poor old man to die?" This was clearly the "bad cop" routine.

"Because you and I both know whose body that is. You and I both know why I did nothing. I can be arrested for manslaughter. I can be arrested for assisted suicide as well. If you don't hear my story, no one will know anything." She spoke calm, rehearsed. She awaited this for a long time.

"Correct me if I'm wrong, but this man here hasn't been identified. You're telling me you want your statement to give this man an identity no one else has? Dragging yourself into a case like this is very risky for you, young lady."

"I'm going to not only identify him, I'm going to give you repeated proof that he existed in this country, and I will tell you why he wanted to be dead."

The man's breath smelled of coffee and sleepless nights when he sighed out. There was clearly more important cases for him to work on, and getting her to admit she was a bystander was his motive. She wanted nothing more than to make this story matter. "Miss, this would be much easier on you if you forget it. Assisted suicide is a worse crime. Honesty is important, but this man was a bum, not worth jail time for you. You have a life, he doesn't."

"He wasn't a bum…He was a painter. He painted my world."

Suicide of Maximus Thenes, supposed painter.

This story is certainly not mine. I'll merely begin it with how I met the man. I'm very well off, as you see, Sarah Fehrfinch, daughter of Alexander Fehrfinch. I've lived a pedigree life from day one, in sweet Los Angeles, California. I recently graduated from high school, and so my father suggested I go abroad or something like that.

That's what landed me at the Marriott on March 22, 2015, one year ago. I had been staying in Portland, studying under this piano player, Robert-something. I wanted to become a pianist, you see, and this man was getting paid well by my father to teach me. This would eventually get me to perform my piano all over Asia. My father wanted this very much.

It was on this day on March 22 that I met Maximus. Maxie, as he greeted me with. I was wearing a black dress, walking down to the studio on Fifth, where I would meet my instructor. As I was passing by, this very grungy, disheveled man looked up at me. He was clearly homeless, but his sign said, "Recovering millionaire, spare a coin to soothe my withdrawals." That was a gas. I certainly had no interest in this man's tall tales. I kept on walking and ended up at my piano studio and began to play.

Not later, Robert (I still forget his last name) came down the stairs. He told me my playing was beautiful. He sat down next to me and began to play "Ode to Joy," maybe a few Mozart works. He kept staring at my fingers, wrapping his over them when he thought I needed instruction. It was typical tutoring until my hour was up.

I'm not going to say he raped me; that's certainly not what happened. He kissed me, yes, he kissed me when I left, kissed me when I was outside, kissed me repeatedly. I had no interest, but I was groomed to deal with men like this. Sit pretty until he stops, don't make a word. I hadn't left the studio. He was just enjoying me out in front of it.

If any witness tells you I cried, you better cut that off the record. No one was there to stop it, so I'm not going to mention it. Yes, I cried, but not because of him. I cried because of my father's decision, this pianist in particular. He expected it to go smoothly, and we'd be married, and I'd lose all hope of becoming anything other than a housewife. I suppose having an opinion isn't for rich girls.

I wasn't paying attention to when it ended. All I knew was I was crying and being carried somewhere. I saw the blood, I saw the man fall, I saw him being kicked and maimed, but I didn't know who had done it. I didn't want the man dead, just to stop what he was doing. I don't think I'll ever forgive Max for hurting that man so badly.

The rugged dirty hands placed me down before my hotel, sitting on the bench in front of the garden. My eyes were too watery to get a good look at who it was. At that time, I only heard his voice responding to my bawls.

"Hush, hush, ma'am. You are safe, I am safe to you. This city, it's not so well for women at night. I'm sorry this man, he done these things to you." His accent was thick and Brazilian. His English was rusty. I remember I was more terrified that he thought it was a street attack.

"D-did you kill that man? I wasn't being attacked, he was just doing as my father asked, I suppose," I responded brokenly between cries.

"The man, his life not worth enough to hurt such a portrait. You are very beautiful, and it is not his beauty. He have no place to give you this pain he give you." He was at eye level with me, trying to convince me what happened was not proper.

I saw his eyes, dark and almost gray, eyes of a long life. His hair was gone except for his long beard. This was the "recovering millionaire" I'd seen this morning. I did what I didn't expect. I laughed. Midcry I laughed at seeing his wrinkly face. He then laughed too, his mouth opening and his few remaining teeth dangling as if they'd jump out anytime. I loved hearing him laugh, because he laughed whenever I did.

Wait a second. Are you telling me that you were aware of the murder of Robert Macindash and you didn't tell anyone? He had a family!

Oh yes, Macindash was his name! I suppose you worked that case? I'm terribly sorry that his wife and children have to learn he died after raping an eighteen-year-old girl. How cruel.

After laughing for what felt like hours, I took in his appearance. His skin was barely attached, he was old, and he was homeless. This was no way for my hero to live. I asked him if he'd like to stay the night in my room. It was a villa at the top floor, so he'd live in style. He said he couldn't possibly allow that, but I insisted.

It was raining that night. I brought him up to my room, and I forced him to take a shower and waited patiently for him to return so he could tell his story to me. I'd never been so excited in my life. He finished and exited, his beard being held in several hair ties. Seeing him cleaned up, he deserved so much more respect. I wish the way anyone saw him was like that first day. I wanted to learn so much from him.

He told me his name was Maximus Thenes, and he was born in a small village in Brazil called Paracuru. He was born to a fisherman on October 17, 1947. His mother was French. She was tied down to her husband, who was stern and strict. He wanted his son to become a big fisherman and that he would go up to America to try and get on as a commercial fisherman. His mother was a huge art enthusiast, big follower of Picasso and Zdzisław Beksiński and other surrealist artists. He told me she liked to imagine a world that was odd and misshapen.

His earliest memory was when he was seven, and he was holding his mother's hand. She spoke to him in French, and his father spoke Spanish. His first memory was creating a sentence out of both languages, learning he was bilingual. For some reason, that stuck out to him, and that was what he told me. He remembered they were walking along the beach. He smelled the saltwater and the gulls. The sun was still high. He would go on to paint that later in his work *Day at Sea*. The painting is him and his mother standing on a four-foot island in the middle of the ocean. It really is beautiful.

For the rest of his youth, he only mentioned his father in a negative light. His father only married his mother for her beauty, her exoticism. He didn't expect her to be a strange woman, a woman who would be called crazy. She loved to learn. He described his mother as his "glowing inspiration," and he even titled a portrait of her that. He painted for the first time when he was eleven. It was a summer monsoon, and he decided he would paint his father, holding a hook and throwing heaps of fish into a boat. It wasn't a good painting, he told me, but it was his first. Apparently his father burned it because it made him look like a poacher rather than a great fisherman, which was his intention. He got beat after that. Every time his father was angry, it was at him. He told me he was thankful for this, because his mother didn't have the will to survive the beatings any longer.

He read his mother's painting books often. He painted his first masterpiece when he was sixteen. The story behind it is beautiful, and I think I'll tell that one.

It was a rainy morning still. His father had been trying to teach him to be a man. Painting was stupid and wouldn't make any money. Of course Max was a grand fisherman, better than his father. Max painted lots of fishing-themed paintings. One of them was *Hook for Teeth*, a portrait of a man as a fish and he had rusty hooks for teeth. Anyway, it was a rainy morning, and Max was playing this bamboo pipe he fashioned on the patio. He told me the sun was kissing him all over, and the wind was hugging him. There was a large heron down by the beach he could see.

The same night he was beaten savagely by his father for starting the painting of a heron. It was supposedly a beautiful colorful painting of the bird, colored on stretched-out bedsheets. His father burned it. He was their family martyr and would continue to be.

Heron at Sea was his first published work. It was a heron made out of blue-and-green plants, trying to stand in an endless black ocean. The bird is struggling to stand and flailing its wings, but the black sea is giving it nowhere to stand. The painting portrays his terror and shock at that age, and it's a painting I'd love to own. That painting was what brought money to his home.

He wasn't known yet. The painting was bought by a rich native, never to see a museum. The money paid was enough to buy his father a new boat and his mother a bigger house, but that was the end of it. Max never got rich until he was in his midtwenties.

At nineteen, Max was married. He married a woman that he didn't know, the daughter of one of his father's friends. His mother said that she was beautiful, and they would be happy together. His mother throughout his childhood was a wonderful mother. He didn't learn that she was delusional. She would always talk about things he didn't understand, how voices had brought him to her. She was very religious but didn't speak of any godly religion. It was when he was nineteen that his mother thought her work was done and swam out into the ocean. She drowned to escape her husband.

When this happened, he fled to Argentina. He got a little apartment with Daphne, his arranged wife. She was a boring woman who didn't care much for his company. He learned to love her deeply. He painted her in different ways every day, but she hated every one of them. It was his twentieth birthday, and he painted her staring out of their bedroom window. He painted her without a head, and in place of her head was a milk carton filled with water. Every part of her was very detailed, but her head was a gallon carton of water, half filled. He never told me what it meant, but he titled it *The Medicine Woman*.

The Medicine Woman was a hit with the Argentine public. It got copied three times, and he made a good amount of money off it. Daphne divorced him a year later, taking a majority of his money.

He never had children, and he continued painting without much qualm till he was thirty. It was 1977, and Argentina was mad with nationalism and war. The dictatorship of Jorge Videla had many people in terror. Max told me many of his friends were against the dictatorship, and one was kidnapped and assumed dead. That was his friend Carlos, which would become one of the returning characters in his paintings. Carlos was always painted with a sewn mouth but a halo over him. In 1978 he published *Guns Are People*. It was a portrait of the dictator looking over an automated fish processing plant, except human bodies hung from the hooks. Carlos was being skinned in the background, his eyes tearing up and screams coming from his sewn mouth. This made him one of the most notorious men in Argentina.

He left the country and went back to Brazil in 1978, shortly after producing his painting. The money was flowing in, as the painting was copied several times and used as a political statement for the country's dictatorship. He moved back in with his father, who had been humbled by old age. He told me he never hated his father, even through the beatings, because he was not the father he chose to remember. He remembered the father that got shot for harboring a political fugitive, which happened in 1979.

His father was painted. Another grisly painting was done in 1980 of his father. The father's face was cut in half. Half was his father, a bullet placed in his smiling head. The other half of the face was Carlos, sewn mouth and eyes and all that. This painting was titled *The End of It All*, and it was the last released painting. It was global. I'm sure you've seen it. He made money off it, enough to hire bodyguards. This was when he became a millionaire, he said. He moved up to America like his father hoped he would.

He bought a mansion in Los Angeles and got married again. This woman only wanted him for his talent, but he simply wouldn't paint her. He refused. He said she wanted an older him. For twenty years he lived off the royalties of *The End of It All* until he couldn't anymore. He hitchhiked up to Portland and stayed there for sixteen years, living in hotels at first, until he ran out of money. Lost his ID in several muggings and now he is dead.

Wow…just wow. I know that was a summary, and I promise you that this man will be identified. Continue?

Well, after he told me his story, which mind you took several days, he said he would like to paint me. He didn't want to paint me how I am now. He said that when he saw me look down at him and chuckle at his sign, in comparison to me crying, that was what he wanted to paint. He wanted to paint rich in peril. He wanted to paint crying and happiness and everything my face has shown him.

I still remember the butterflies I got when he painted me that first time. My father had called to tell me the pianist had been murdered. I faked shock, and that was the end of it. After the call ended, I sat in a wooden stool, and Max got to work. I provided him with canvases and paints and everything he would need. He was my hero.

While he painted, I talked. I talked about my father and how he was always preoccupied, how my mother had been dead after I was born, never told how she died. I talked about my brothers, who had gone to Ivy League schools, lost touch with. I told him about how my father liked to beat my spirit down, then raise it down. When I learned horseback riding, my father told me I'd fail at it until I was very, very good at it, then told me he lied to me all those times. That was what he did.

My portrait was beautiful. It was my face but golden. My skin was entirely a shiny golden, painful-looking color, and I was crying chromey silver tears. I held my hands to my face, one of my gold hands covering half of my face. Robert was painted as a red demonic figure, mismatched limbs and green blood all over him. He was in the background, lying belly up. From the doorway in the background stood a blue rendition of Carlos. It was the most beautiful painting I'd ever seen, and I cried looking at it. I still have it hung in my apartment, and you're very welcome to see it if you need proof.

To remove me from any ties to the murder, my father suggested I return home. So I did, leaving Maximus to his own devices. I lived happily. I hid the painting from my father. It was several months of living as a rich teenager that I couldn't stand, so I took a plane back here to Portland and sought out Max.

Max was still begging, but in a different part of Portland now. I found him, and he pretended not to know me. He changed his sign, and it was saddening to meet him there.

"Max. I've come back, I need to have you safe."

"No, miss, you are fine by yourself, no need of an old man like me."

"Maximus Thenes, the greatest South American painter of my time, says I'm fine alone. Max, you need to become known, show people you're not dead." I spoke, hoping not to closed ears.

The sun shone bright on that day three months ago. A woman in a silk dress speaking with a homeless great painter that no one knew was still alive. His head was down, and I saw a tear fall from his beaten eyes. First one tear, then a second. He kept crying, and I kept observing, knowing that it would be explained to me like it had before.

"I wait so long for someone to understand, but no one has listened. I have been given enough, I do not need more from you," he said, weary lips quivering, his gray eyes avoiding my gaze.

"What do you want, Max? I can give you anything."

He waited a long, long time to respond. He waited until weeks later, while he sat laying in my chair. He became the father I never had for two months, living and laughing and loving me like the daughter he never had. I will remember those times forever, but those are my tales, not yours. The only thing he wanted was to see his mother again.

He painted for the last month of his life. Those paintings are in my apartment that I'm going to give you the key to. The largest canvas in the room is a copy of the mural he was painting when he died. It is titled *From Berth to Birth*, and it is the most gorgeous painting *you* will ever see.

He painted his mother sitting cross-legged, half of her face being made of cigarette boxes. She sat in the middle of the painting, and a large rifle made out of foliage stretches across the background of the canvas. I'm painted golden in the far right corner, and Carlos is painted on the far left. Carlos's tan face is curled into a smile, and his sewn lips are open. I'm crying my silver tears. His father and the dictator and the heron are all placed on the mural. In the right corner, next to me, he painted his only self-portrait. He painted himself in hyper detail, down to his missing teeth and highlight of his baldness. His hand is on my shoulder, and he is smiling. It made me cry when I first saw it.

He finished that painting four days ago. He told me his life was complete. I said that I knew. He told me he thought he was dying of cancer; he could hardly breathe, and there was a lump on his chest that startled him. He said he wouldn't go to the doctor no matter what I said. He told me that he would go to the bad part of town, and he would paint his mural over war and crime. That's what he had been doing his whole life, and he wanted to run from criminals one last time.

That's what he did—forgive me for tearing up. I went without him knowing. I watched him paint. He was as skilled with spray paint as he was with canvas. On that alley wall you will find the majority of that mural painted, only I am missing, and I think it is best that way. They didn't notice me when they found him, and they never will. They pushed him back and forth. He wouldn't have it and swore to them he would continue his painting, and they had to leave. That's when the bullet was put through his head, two more for spite.

That's what happened, Officer. That's all I'm going to recount. He had no relation to me on paper. He needed an identity, and now I've given you one.

End of report.

* * *

The paintings were recovered and placed in the Brazilian museum of fine art. The mural was never finished. Sarah's report was published, but when further questioned, she only answered that "He was the man that painted my universe."

SIDE EFFECTS OF OBSESSION

Better hold on to your teeth, kiddies, 'cause you'll want to rip 'em out.

Amy. What was she about? A creation of twisted beauty, a mirror painted black, still shining against the darkness. How ironic. She was a sad girl that sat outside of Walgreens at night, two different-colored shoes. All she ever did was smoke all the time I saw her.

This here is why people tell me I'm crazy. I get the idea, just the fabrication of somebody, somebody that means something. I get locked into this idea there's a cleanliness in all the filth. Are you going to find a block of gold in shit? No, that's how it tends to go.

It still exists, though. If you believe hard enough, anything is spotless. Probably why all the goddamn perverts and murderers in this city don't feel bad. They believe hard enough that what they're doing is okay. She was really clean, though, truly spotless, merely tried to look grungy. The illusion of filth. Dark scarlet lipstick, the way her crowish hair hung over those blood-colored lips. She was beautiful in every morbid way imaginable.

Anyway, I'd be out at night on these long walks. Sometimes out till the break of dawn, sometimes not back till the morning. It's what you do when you can't sleep. I'd be nicking hard, struggling to find my lighter. Go out and search for cigarette butts sometimes. Had a fight with Mom. The insufferable woman wouldn't stop telling me to get some rest and get an education and move out and do everything I couldn't possibly do.

I'd walk, waiting for total darkness to glue me to the picture of night, like some magazine cutout in a goth scrapbooker's dream work. The whole area would become pitch-black. The bushes, the trees, cats, dead birds, people, every entity in the world will be dark and black and unseen. All of it is dark except the open highway.

Night is beautiful. Normally there's lights and cars and traffic and coffee and drama, but at this hour, it all just...goes away. The only observers of this nightly emptiness are the high, powerful, ever-observing streetlights and me, their humble mortal pupil. They still give out colorful orders even when all their servants are asleep in garages around the world. They have no idea what to do with their time but continue the commands to all those around to gaze them. It makes me think, the privileged don't know they're privileged. When there's no one to order around, they just keep ordering whoever's listening.

These guardians have protected her every night. Shining against her long pale arm, green and red and yellow curling off her skin. The lights bounce off the arm leading down to thin, long elegant fingers, cupped around a cigarette blocking the wind. Breathing between her lips her death, the death making her beauty grow as she danced closer toward it.

That's how I met her. I met the idea of her. Every night as I'd travel down that same road, she would be my guiding light. Seeing her breath in that stale air was my goal of the evening. Light can't see itself shine; it's moving too fast.

I can remember well the first time I talked to her. It was cold. She was wearing a black knitted skirt and a long sweater. I sometimes went into the store and bought a tea or a beer or something to give me an excuse to be there. The cashier at this hour grew to know me, grew to expect me. Tonight was no different. I bought a can of piss and left without a word. Besides "thank you," of course, but that's two.

I sat there, next to the trash can, sipping the god-awful drink. I studied her with my right eye, analyzing her every movement. It was her fifth cigarette of the night, and I had watched her smoke every one. Something about her heavy breathing made me excited to be alive, gave me purpose to be there that night. Soon, her pale feature-less face hinted in my direction, her dark-green eyes meeting mine for a fraction of a second.

Our first meeting was worth a sigh. Her sharp lips parting for a beautiful moment to let out a barely audible exhale. Smoke lifting from her lungs and escaping into the atmosphere, taking with them a piece of her existence. She inhaled again, looking in my direction, as if breathing in my being, my feelings, and more importantly, her opinion of me.

This woman did not play hard to get. She invented the game. I was nothing in her universe. I was just another spectral body floating by her shining vortex on this cold night, hoping that some slight chaotic force of gravity could bring our systems together. I could have remained that nothing, I could have flew on by without any force applied, but I had to make myself gravitate to her.

A thousand years stood between my words and her ears. Without my consent, my shaking fingers reached out to beckon for a drag. The distance slowly lifted between our hands, and I held the stick to my mouth. Her fingers were painted over bitten-down nails, her anxious hands returning to her pack of Marlboros.

In that moment I tried so hard to understand her. I tasted the remnants of her waxy lipstick on the filter, learning the texture and absorbing it into my memory. A chalky, dry feeling, very dark and *very* red. Her beauty was caused by a deep hatred. The hatred was for what? I didn't have an answer for a very long time.

I say a lie is just a life that hasn't existed yet. There's nothing anyone can say or do that hasn't been thought out yet. There's no fake doctor or fake FBI agent that doesn't have the capability to be real. We put on these facades to impress those we need to impress and tell them the truth when the lie's life is dead. It's the way of the world, but this woman was on a separate planet entirely. Every motion she had was honest, angry, and cynical but honest. There was nothing about her that had no purpose, even down to the black shoelaces on her beat-up purple-and-green hiking boots.

There we stood, her crouching on the wall, me leaning against it. Four feet, seven inches away from each other, separated by nothing but a fear of breaking the silence. So we decided not to. We just kept looking at the world through a foggy, broken window we wouldn't look through any other time of night.

I felt her gaze on me during every inhale, her eyes tracing the smoke down to my lungs. Her green eyes filled my chest to the core, feeding off my oxygen before leaving out the way they came, taking with them a little piece of me, and replacing it with a piece of her. It was an astounding feeling, feeling every emotion someone could give to you in seconds, all the pain, all the torment, all the rare happiness, all of it a gorgeous lie that was yet to come true. Her death flowed over me, and I gladly accepted it.

"The name's Richard," I muttered, a nervousness hiding under my chilly, stoic demeanor. I'd like to imagine it was cool and stoic, but I know it wasn't.

"Oh," she rolled off her tongue, a ball of smoke carrying the name she had heard and rejecting it immediately. No sweetness concealed her disinterest. It was earnest rejection, the kind you should let slide, the kind which should make someone stop pursuing. The kind that would make her seem like any other emo bitch in the country, but the kind that made me want to keep going.

I desperately wanted to hear more of her spiteful, sharp voice. It's the voice of someone who'd been beaten, crushed, knocked out and divorced at the same time, and stood back up saying "Fuck you" to the turn of events. She still had a sour tone but a hint of sweetness that was once there. She was so very worth my everything, and I gladly gave it to her.

She eventually put out her cigarette, and I eventually finished my piss water, and I walked home. I knew she'd be in the same spot tomorrow. She knew I'd come back and fake not being infatuated with her.

I like to think of Amy as an angel. She wasn't in the least. If she was, she ripped off her wings and spat on them a long time ago. She was the most gorgeous time bomb I ever met. Tricky feelings like that, that hurt you really bad. Emotions we all get but don't put into words because it would hurt too bad. The emotion that snares your personality but forces you to travel on into the world you hate so much. Words can't trap those kinds of emotions. They're the kind that have to detonate and hit everything in the vicinity. Words are just the middleman. Emotions are the hard, unrefined product that dealers load onto trucks heading to the consumers.

We smoked together for a long time after that. She always had a cigarette laid on the trash can for me. She always pretended she didn't leave it there. I still didn't know her name at that time. This kept on a pattern for two and a half weeks, every night more ravishing than the last.

One night she didn't show up. She hadn't been absent since I had first seen her there so long ago. It was as if she had betrayed our unspoken promise. I waited a long time. I went in, bought a six-pack, and returned to the outside. I drank half of it, waited another hour, drank the other half, and waited another hour. I was angry. I was angry she hadn't showed up. I was furious at myself for hoping she'd be there. I was angry at everything.

As I fumed in my buzzed rage, like a vampire she strutted into view from the night. Her legs were long. I'd never seen her stand. My eyes led up to her face, and I saw an irksome expression planted on it.

"You're sitting in my spot," she uttered. Imagining her tapping her foot was fun at the time, so I kind of chuckled trying to see what her showing emotion would be like.

"It's almost sunrise, doll. Where the hell were you?" My first real sentence to her, and it had to be the most offensive thing I could think of.

"It took you inebriation to finally talk to me?" she scoffed out. It was as deadpan as all her other sentences but more disappointed somehow.

"How the hell am I supposed to? You're intimidating."

"And you're a creep."

"You're some goth chick that hangs out and chain-smokes."

"And you're the guy that joins me! What's your fascination with me?" She raised her voice a little more at this, which amused me.

"I'm not sure yet, what's your obsession with being here every night?"

"That's not your business."

"Why can't it be?"

She huffed and stood in the spot I usually stood in, lighting up just before the break of dawn. I was still buzzed, so my observation was a little more obvious. She turned her head away from me, pretending I wasn't there.

"Can I bum a drag? I'm out."

"No. You're drunk, and I don't like drunks."

I stood up, which at the time was more challenging than I had expected, and leveled myself with her eyes. She still kept her head turned away from me, which was fine because she had wonderful ears. I wasn't worthy of her sight, but I persisted anyway.

"You're bothering me, politely fuck off," she mumbled.

She sounded hurt, damaged beyond repair. Her cover had been chipped, her shield was down, and I could have learned anything about her I wanted at that moment. Instead I stood up and gestured to where I was sitting. She didn't move, so I walked to the left and tried my best to face her, only to have her hands launch over her face in defense. It looked like she expected me to hit her, and I felt so sorry that was her reaction.

I merely stood there, staining her essence with my booze breath, dying to see her react in some way to my shift. There was none. She just sat down and lit her smoke like every other night, except the light was finding its way out. I felt dreadfully exhausted, and so I went home. I walked down the street, taking the set of curves to my driveway and pushing my key into the latch.

There were two things I thought at that moment. Hatred and love, both of which were very blurred due to my intoxication. I guess they were blurred always; that's how our relationship had been. I didn't sleep. I just sat on my couch and stared at the ceiling. About thirteen minutes later, I heard a light rapping on the door.

I peered through the viewer to see the girl looking at the door. Her mascara was running, and her hands were jittering like crazy. I slid the door open, barely enough for her to talk through.

"You never answered me! You never told me why you're obsessed with me." She spoke shakily, as if my answer marked whether or not she'd continue breathing.

"Who said I was obsessed with you?" A tinge of hate in my throat.

She pushed the door open, open into the small home I owned, open into the life I had created around myself to shield the outside world. She opened the door and walked into my life on her own coalition. I beat her at her own game. She pressed me against the wall, her breath bobbing with fresh wails.

I'd like to be romantic and say this was the moment I fell in love with her, but that was not what it was. This was the climax to a story I'd been writing every night for the past many weeks. This was the end, the ever-ending resolution that would inevitably be our downfall. This was the beautiful, Brechtian end of the story I'm telling you, hidden cautiously in the middle.

"What do you want? Do you want my body? Do you want me to do whatever you want? Do you want to kill me or rape me or whatever it is in your sick mind? Do you want to scar me? Why don't you answer me!" Her tears dropped with every syllable, each tear holding a separate thought. "Well, here I am! You won! Do what you want, I don't care anymore. Just make me good for something!"

For the first real time in the nonexistent relationship, I felt sorry for her. She had always been this stale, unmoving force driving my pursuit. She wasn't human to me. She was an idol I could have worshipped, and these were the tears of God drowning my Garden of Eden. I slowly raised my arms to her shoulders, pushing her off lightly and guiding her to the couch. I told her the only thing I wanted was her to be happy, and that would require her sleeping right on that couch and being happy in the morning. I didn't care where she needed to be, but it wasn't safe having her outside like this. It was plenty light outside, and it wasn't the most dangerous part of the world, but I know she thought it was, and she needed to think she was safe.

I suppose that was our first date. Her refusing to sleep, so instead I got out the brandy. At 6:39 a.m., I drank an entire bottle of brandy with a girl who's name I didn't know. First it was me who got up, noticing how she twitched every time I moved. See, any therapist would tell you that when someone is having a nervous breakdown, the last thing they need is alcohol, but I'm not a therapist. I'd had a bottle, and I figured brandy would cure her of her ailments.

The birds began to chirp soon, screaming to the heavens their desire to come home. When you think about birds like that, their singing ain't so happy. Glass and glass and glass and glass and eventually she talked. It wasn't talking really. She mumbled and kind of wheezed. After a bit, she said thank you.

"I think I'm in the wrong. Been stalking you for a month and you say thank you?" I stumbled out, the booze taking more effect. The fact I was still alive was astounding.

"I really am thankful, kinda always wanted a creep. Daddy tells ya when you're little not to talk to strangers. When Daddy's not there, who are you supposed to talk to?" She laughed at this, sitting halfway up. Her poufy sleeves hung on her slender arms like loose skin, and her arms were riddled with cuts and bruises.

"That's fucked." My tongue tried to catch it before it flew off, but it was already off the runway. A bird flaps quietly, dying in its nest, better fate than most poor flying creatures deserve.

"Hey, man, so are you. Chasing a young girl every night. Smoking her cigarettes, stealing her air."

"Maybe you could quit if it bothers you so—"

"You could just kiss me or…or something. I don't know why yer even…yer even talking to me."

I sighed. I would've gladly taken up on her offer a few days ago, and the alcohol sitting on my gut screamed for me to meet her request. I didn't want to, though. I hadn't had any responsibility before in my life, and I just caught my savior on her leap from paradise. I need to be mature.

She flipped her wrist back and forth, as if it could fall off at any second. Any smart person would not let her keep drinking. Any smart person would think this small woman couldn't handle it in the state she was in. I was not a smart person. I was an infatuated boring young man that had done nothing with his life besides not sleeping for a good portion of it. She kept studying her arms, her eyes fluttering occasionally.

So I had another drink. It was about seven thirty, and there was nothing better to do. She talked for a little bit about this bear she saw when she was little, a grizzly bear. I couldn't care less. I was getting sad. Really sad, so I thought I'd be able to sleep, all sauced up and sad like that. Closed my eyes, heard her say something again and passed out.

I'd love to say I woke up, and the birds were chirping, and the sky was singing, and she was wearing a beautiful ball gown, and we got married or some shit like that. That's not how it went. I woke up at three in the afternoon, and she left a note telling me to never talk to her again. She cleaned up the empty bottle, which I suppose she finished that morning, and left. I had the chance of a lifetime and shot it down. I could've caused her pleasure and made her feel human and make her feel beautiful, but I chose not to. This was all that I thought in that morning, the thoughts of a hungover man infatuated.

I tried to incorporate her into my day thoughts too. Tired mechanic, exhausted engineer, sleepless sappy sucker. I couldn't help but see her in everything I did. It sounds cliché, but that's how it is, you know? Being in love is half actual love and the other half being pissed you can't focus on anything else. It's a horrid emotion, and I'm glad I have nothing to do with it now.

It was a while, a while before I saw her again. I couldn't stand rejection, who can? So I did like she said and moved on for a week or two. Spent every day thinking I'd see that crow's nest hair from a street corner, excited to see those pale snaky arms wherever I looked. It wasn't to be for those days, but I eventually remembered I didn't know her name. It's impossible to fall in love without knowing their name. That's why I say it ain't love now.

I looked for her now. Looked and looked in streets, knowing she would be in the area. It wasn't until I was driving around the neighborhood a week later when I drove past this old house having a garage sale. It was in the beat-up part of town, a half mile from my house. They weren't selling much, a few CDs, old clothes, stuff like that. A few minutes into the piles and I was already done. This was luck that saved me, luck that caused this to happen. If my head were ten degrees to the right, I wouldn't have seen her. I didn't want to see her, but there framed in the windowsill across the cracked concrete was the queer woman. Her boney, scarred arm resting against it, her head tilted, and she was sleeping. I wanted to knock, but I didn't. I didn't do that. What I did was I did the worst thing anyone could do. I waited until she left.

I was waiting in my well-earned shitty car, and I waited until she left her house. This was until night, and I then learned she kept doing her nightly routine. I didn't jump out of my car immediately, waited until she was at her driveway, dressed in these weird black overall things. They were cute but horribly large on her. Her face wasn't one of surprise but of disappointment.

There was no reason to say anything. I walked next to her for a while. She saw me, didn't walk faster or slower or yell. I realized this was a bad idea. I was a creep following a girl at night because of some infatuation. Cue the screaming activists. That's the thing about it. It's not ever mutual. That's why people bitch, because they don't understand because they don't feel it. I care for someone, she hates my guts, and I would be dead if she had a weapon.

"What do you want?" she said after she figured out I wouldn't leave.

"I want to at least know your name."

"It's Amy. Now leave, I'm trying hard to hate you."

"Beautiful name for a beautiful girl." She laughed. Her laugh was honest. It told me she had a reason to not believe this.

"I've heard it. You probably symbolize me or some shit, all creepy stalkers do. Now leave. My dad used to say beautiful name for beautiful girl when he'd pick up chicks all the time. Not worth my time."

I exhaled every grain of sand that was falling from my broken hourglass. Again, this was an awkward situation. "Listen. You're fucked up, your life is fucked up, I'm fucked up for wanting to be part of it. What isn't fucked up is how I feel about you. I've seen you sad as hell every night, if not in my dreams. I'm not saying I wanna be with you, I'm saying let me be part of your life so maybe I can decide whether or not you're worth it."

"Fine. I'm probably going to always hate you, but I'll let you hang around. You seem the least creepy, just kinda pathetic."

"Thank you, I certainly am pathetic."

That was the start. All it took was that little line. She laughed. She chuckled. She went into full-on belly-aching laughter. That laughter, that joy kept going for six months, six months of constant bitching. Constant aching and self-hatred and togetherness that lasted a little nothing. Everyone likes to think of a relationship as an infinity, but Amy and I liked to think of time as nothing and loved to say our relationship would never exist outside of time, so why should it exist in time?

She was very self-contradictory. This one time we talked about the ethics of eating dogs. She told me she didn't mind if people ate dogs. "It's no different than eating people."

I laughed, saying, "Oh, it's okay to eat people then?"

She said, "Absolutely. Romance is just a constant competition to breed and create things to eat other things." She said you're constantly feeding off each other's emotions. Children feed off your guidance. Children eat, and you eat their happiness. When you're low, you gnaw on your lover's bones a little and chipper up. She looked at the world with cynical eyes, and I loved it.

There was this one time, I took her to the aquarium. It was a month or two into our relationship. She started staying with me. She made it okay for me to sleep. I took her there, another night of watching her sleep in my bed. Just as good as sleep. Anyway, I took her to the aquarium, and we were looking at the sharks. Amy saw this little pufferfish. She said she loved how it could protect itself even though it was so little. She just didn't wanna leave, so I stayed with her. She was there about an hour, and I couldn't help but watch her childlike enthusiasm. She'd squeak every time it blew itself up. At some point we moved on and watched the guy feed the seals. Here they fed the seals live fish and tossed 'em right in there. Amy saw one fish she liked, said it had a special glow. For a while it swam around, the seals paying more attention to the schooling fish. Needless to say, the fish got eaten, and she collapsed. She could get attached to stuff like that, fish that she liked. She was bawling, and I took her down by the tunnel away from the fish, and she cried on and on.

"T-these little fish. They don't all get to protect themselves. Why can't they all be pufferfish? Why do the pretty ones have to go just because they can't defend themselves? Why is nature so cruel!" she sputtered, while I cradled her. She was nineteen, still acted like a little girl sometimes.

"It doesn't matter if they're pretty. Some fish are meant to be food. Some of 'em are meant to not be able to protect themselves. They just can't. Even the puffer fish has predators, everything has predators. One day everything dies, you know this better than me."

She insisted I take her right there. Told me she didn't want to end up like a fish, didn't want her last memory to be crying over fish. The fish didn't get the chance to cry, and so she was lucky and wanted to express that luck. It was a weird day, but those were the kinds of thoughts she had. She said she hated me more than anything during it, didn't care about the occasional person walking by.

That was our thing. She never said she loved me. She only said it once. She would always say she hated me, whenever a normal person would say they loved you. I was so used to it. At first it put me off. We were always like that, so snide with each other. I was always the good cop, and she was Hitler. That's how our relationship worked, and I loved it—correction, hated it.

She told me one time why she said that. She said that was how her dad used to say it. Her dad never said he loved her, because hate was stronger and love was so close to it. She said, you're always thinking about someone, you wanna be near them and touch 'em a lot. You wanna know everything about 'em, and being away from them just makes the feeling worse. No different than having a huge grudge on them. Her dad put it that way, before he died and left her the house. She sold it after moving in with me.

Why am I droning on and on about that? I'm not quite sure. I don't know why she meant so much to me. She was like a sister when we weren't being a couple. We were usually not a couple. She was moody and boring majority of the time. I just liked watching her, though, as if she would disappear if I took my eyes away.

I never had a woman in my life besides my mom. Crazy old bat, talking about her knitting and how she saw a squirrel, talking to me like I was eleven. It was nice that she thought I didn't grow up, and maybe I truly didn't, but I liked pretending I did. That's what Amy gave me.

Amy never had a man in her life. All her life, she grew up with a crazy freemason. He was secretive and rich. She never told me about her mom. Every time I asked, she just distracted me. That was how she was, very strategic. She said her dad wasn't an asshole. He didn't abuse her. He didn't hurt her emotionally. He just let her be. She told me that she would've rather him be an abuser, because at least she would have mattered. He left her everything, as a kind of apology for not being there for her in life.

It took a while for her to tell me why she was there at night all the time. Those cold nights, those warm nights, those nights she would be there smoking until dawn. I expected something poetic. It was a cold night. We were sitting in the bathroom, making a poor man's sauna. You turn the shower on, and you close the door and wait. That's how hard it is, no need for expensive rooms and shit.

She leaned over to me, setting her chin on my knee and started talking. She talked at first about fish, about how we evolved from them. About how we spent eighty-five million years of evolution just to become a sad girl that goes to Walgreens at night hoping she'd meet someone worth her while. "You know, what would our ancestors think? That one day, some 310 billion days in the future, there will be my great-times-a-million granddaughter sitting, killing herself with smoke outside of a really fancy cave filled with luxuries, waiting for someone to feel special."

"Really? That's why you were there all the time?"

"I think it is. At first I wasn't sure why. I kinda tried to suspend the fact that I was lonely. I didn't know I was waiting for you, and maybe I wasn't. Maybe I'll find a better reason in the future, but right now, I hate you more than anything in the world, and that's probably why. That one day I'll find someone that means more to me than my fucked-up dad."

That was a weird night. We kept talking like that. I droned on and on about how crazy my mom was, how I knew her when I was a kid, and how she had to break as I grew up. I grew up to stop sleeping. She asked me why I rarely slept. I told her I just haven't found a reason, nothing to dream about. Until I met her, I didn't sleep until I passed out, and now I didn't sleep at all.

She said she was happy I didn't sleep. It killed my filter. She hated phony people, hated those people that filter their words. Words have to be raw so that people know what you're talking about. What you're really talking about, not what you want people to think you're talking about.

You might be asking, dear reader, how does it end? I'd love to say, "Of course, it didn't. I'm still with her, and we're so very happy and all of that." But that's not true. We dated for six months. That was our clock, and then she left.

She left me a letter. A letter, and all her hair. She shaved her long, beautiful hair and put it in a bag. She explained in the letter, that with every haircut she wanted to be a different person. That the person she was is attached to the last thing that was attached to her, the single growing piece of her that she could cut off. So she decided to cut me off and wanted me to cut her off. She was convinced she was bad for me, that she was a terrible person, and she was just holding me back from greatness. She left me her hair, just in case I was some freak that wanted to remember who she was. She said that the morning she left me after trying to care for her was the inevitable end of everything. That the her I had manifested would leave the same way she came. She ended the letter with the most gorgeous cursive sentence I'd ever seen.

She simply wrote, "My dear Richard, I'm glad that I was able to cure your slumber, and I will leave you with constant alertness. I love you more than anything, but I wouldn't dare say it while you're awake."

FURY AND FIRE, BUT NO PASSION

There's something floating out in the water. Looks like a piece of paper, shopping receipt or something. A receipt for five boxes of condoms and a bunch of Sudafed. Those tweakers and their sex drive. I swear to god, if everyone knew that about meth, then we'd all be doing it. That's what I think the receipt is for, knowing the neighborhood I'm in. Also considering I'm drinking a beer in the backyard of a burning meth lab with the rotting corpses of two poor souls lying next to five empty boxes of condoms. Doesn't take Sherlock Holmes to figure out why the hell they would pay for something.

I throw a few Coronas in the water from a six-pack found in the fridge. I'm looking at my watch, 9:57 a.m. I'd say I have about five and a half minutes to get out of here until the police notice that a residence is on fire and another ten to decide that it is too much effort to go and check it out. Only people that live in this neighborhood are meth heads and meth dealers, not the good kind either. Just enough time to make a phone call.

I kick off my shoes at the door, noticing the mat is disgusting and I'd rather not wipe my feet on it. I put my shoes back on hastily. I walk past the fly-ridden bedroom and into the kitchen. The couch in the living room is engulfed, I'm assuming from the Molotov, but maybe they have shit insurance. The half-melted dial-up works pretty bad, but I'm able to dial it.

It rings for a bit before that sweet, energetic voice kicks up. "Hey…who's this?"

"Hey, it's Art! You know, from a few days ago, blind date, the one with the really bothersome eyebrows."

"Oooohh, Artemis! Hi there! What's up?" God that voice is so sweet it could've melted my very being. That is actually the phone melting.

"Hey, Hannah! Um, nothing much. I was wondering if you wanted to meet up and do bowling or something later. I hope that ain't too soon to say or nothing, I mean it was only a few days ago we had our first date. But really, it's your choice, I think you might just say no anyway, sorry—"

"Jesus, Art! What are you talking about? Of course. You're a great guy. Is your connection all right, your mic is getting spotty." I reach to the speaker to find the plastic end of the phone lying in a puddle at my feet. The speaker is hanging by a thread, so I just grab it and hold it closer. "Oh, that's better. Anytime you want to swing by will be fine, I have no plans today. I gotta go hop in the shower, though. Just knock whenever."

It's a good thing the call ended then. I don't think I could've handled much more. I was so nervous. Anyway, let's see here. Pull my to-do list out of my jeans. Call Hannah, check. I stumble over to a half-burning table, cross it off the list, and toss the list into the flames. I make sure to say goodbye to the folks and close the door to keep the wind out. The door falls to ashes behind me. They'll have to call a repairman about that.

I ponder the implications of Hannah's message. *Oh, Art, I'm in the shower, knock whenever.* Which door did she mean? No, definitely not, it's only been the second date. I brush the ash off my flannel and head down toward Plaid Pantry. There are a few guys across the road, double teaming a shrub. It's pretty intense, would've been some serious romance in a tree-huggers porno or something, but none of my business. Jesus, I hate this place.

There's this streetcar that runs by this neighborhood. Not through it, but the stop is right by the Plaid, so I'll hop on. Door jingles, my clickity-clackity boots hitting the floor. I grab a coffee, and I stand in the Mexican pastry section. You know, those little yellow-and-red packages, seeming like something out of a nineties commercial. Maybe they had a commercial, but it's like our brains just hone in on that "*I know that from somewhere*" type of feeling when we see it. My brain happens to think of a nineties commercial, though one was probably never made. Anyway, I grab one of those, and I go to pay.

The dude at the counter has a shaved head. Samoan guy, shaved head, weird goatee. I ask for a pack of Camels. He rings it up, $9.58. I scrounge around my seemingly bottomless jeans and hand him a ten. I realize I forgot the money in the bedroom, and it's probably burning with its owners right now. Whatever, it was fake anyhow. Bimbo! That's what they're called.

The streetcar has just filled. People all over it, like usual. This one guy is reading a Dungeons and Dragons strategy guide. He looks about fifty. He isn't the kinda guy that would play it. He's the kinda guy that'll read anything that's put in front of him. I'm guessing his son got involved in some serious nerdiness, and he's trying to relate or something. I know that feeling, when your son doesn't want anything to do with you no matter how hard you try. Really sucks.

Hannah's apartment is a really tall thing. I drove her here last time. I've never seen inside, but I know that it's apartment *117* and that I'm going to knock when I go up there. Hannah was a really pretty doll when I saw her. That kind of curly hair that she hates to see curly but doesn't want to straighten it either, so she just messes with it all the damn time. Either that or she was on cocaine when I met her, very plausible, but she seems like a nice girl. Don't even get me started on those fingernails, oh my goodness. Crazy designs must've taken her like forty hours to make them. She draws 'em like watermelon, green rinds at the base and red with black dots. On her thumb and pinky, she even drew a detailed little ant chewing at the melon. A girl with that kind of dedication is one I need in my life, sweet diggity.

Her floors are separated into letters because the owner likes to be confusing as shit. So the ground floor is labeled "A" on the elevator. But the button still says "G" on it. And the buttons still have the numbers on them. So technically she's on the ninth floor, room 17. Took me a minute to figure out, but now I know. The eighties bar green paint is chipping in the hall she lives in, and her door is a long way down the curvy hallway.

I decide I have to say "knock" as well as knock, so that's interesting. A tall man yelling at a door that he is knocking whilst pummeling it. And somehow we associate this action with hospitality. Here, let me assault your door to alert you I want to steal your time. I hear a chipper *"I'm coming"* from a few feet away, and the most beautiful black mop I've ever seen opens the door, but only a crack.

"Hey, Art, um…Don't come in just yet, maybe wait right there. I'll be ready in a second. It'll be quick, I promise. BRB!"

She says "BRB" just right like that. It disgusts me but is also cute how she just used that unintentionally, and in a little while, I'm going to make a joke about it. Makes me wonder if celebrities ever do that. I can't imagine Samuel L. Jackson saying "LOL" or "LMAO" or any other abbreviation out loud. He does say "muthafucka" a lot. Makes me afraid of saying "What" for the rest of my life. Always afraid that whenever I say "what," he'll pop out from around the corner and blow my brains out. Then clean me up and talk about Jesus. But it's okay. Celebrities aren't real people.

That's funny to think, but what really is real? I'm just as likely to meet a celebrity as the junkie lovers are to give me a jingle and ask for my insurance. Sure, if Mr. Jackson just happened to be in this part of Portland and he happened to walk down this hallway on his way to a *Pulp Fiction* reunion and forgot to grab the gun that wasn't loaded, and if by chance I begged and pleaded to do a play scene and be Mr. I-said-what-too-many-times-so-now-I'm-dead, it could happen. That's nearly impossible, so in my lifetime, it isn't real. So celebrities are not real to me.

All this bullshit going through my nervous head makes the time pass by quickly. I'm sure it's far longer than a second but enough time to notice I smell awful. Mainly like chemicals and a little like smoke. My flannel is covered in ash, but my undershirt is all right. I'll just work up a little flannel-around-the-waist action.

"Ready to go? Where are we going, by the way? You mentioned bowling, but is that a definite or…?" She says "or" as the end of a question. Oh my goodness, the modern appeal.

"Do you want it to be? I suppose it could be, there's bowling not too far from here, just down off Eightieth. A short ride, you see? There's this place you can eat too. They use cucumbers as decorations in their restaurant."

"Well, it sounds like you have a plan in mind. Saucy, let's go." Her watermelon-painted nails hold themselves out to me, lifting me from my crouching position.

I am so happy Phillus set us up. I always hated blind dates. The only one I've gone on was with an actual blind gal, and that didn't work out very well. I'm not too bad looking, but my voice makes me sound like a seventy-five-year-old Vietnam veteran, which is fine if you're into that sort of thing. I don't think she was. Probably why when I called her back seven times, she always hung up.

The streetcar ride is uneventful. She talks a lot about how she wants a tortoise because they live forever. She says, "When I have kids, I ain't passing down a rock or a dress or something breakable. I'm passing down a living thing. Something that'll remember me and will remember my kid and will remember my kid's kid and so on." Every word she says, she'd look me straight in the eye and kinda bounce when she got excited. She's a little thing, so it isn't strange-looking for her to bounce in excitement, not a full bounce, just the uncontrollable hip movements you make when you want someone to understand something straight out of your head. If you've never seen anybody do it, your friends are boring or dumb.

She has on this purple suit thing. It is a dress on the bottom but a fitted suit on the top made of purple denim. I think she made it herself, and it was beautiful on her. I don't wanna get attached to her on the second date, but if she keeps being this interesting, I think I'm gonna.

As we pull up to the bowling alley, I look up at the car and see there are a bunch of birds just lolling there at the top of the streetcar. Reminded me of an old Disney short where a bunch of birds fucked with the elasticity of telephone cords. It would take a hell of a lot of birds to bend a streetcar, but it's possible.

"What are you looking at?"

"Just the birds on the streetcar."

"It's funny how they ride the streetcar too, even though they have wings."

"Never thought of it that way."

"Well, why do you think they are up there?"

"I don't know, probably plotting to take over the moving metal perch."

She kinda chuckles. Not the laugh I was going for, but it was a reaction. I buy the tickets, and then we go and get some shoes. This isn't the fanciest alley, with bowling dying and all. I'm not sure why I wanted to go bowling anyhow. It's just the first thing that popped into my head. So they don't have that many rental shoes. I wasn't sure how they couldn't have her size. Her feet are tiny. I'd say they were probably a 4 in women's, maybe if that. She had on these weird heels, though, so I don't know how they could have a strange set of heels but no bowling shoes. So she got the next size up, which is a 5 in women's. I believe they only cater to women without feet here.

I never was good at bowling. I decide to be a man and go without bumpers. She decides to go without as well, and she actually has skill. The way her arm curves to slide it, how she is already so close to the ground. I guess this is why I've never done well with dates. I'm either talking too much or staring too much.

My turn is up. I got a nothing. I don't know what the words are. On the fourth turn of her getting a 9 or a strike or a spare, she decides to help me. "Start out holding the ball here." Holding my arm back behind me, she holds my wrist until I let go of the ball. She had more instructions while that was occurring, but I couldn't focus. She's got this really nice look about her when she's concentrating or telling you something important. The kind of look where she wants to just think and have you hear it, but words get in the way. "It's that easy!" she says while I managed to knock down a few pins.

"Wow. Thank you very much," I say unintentionally dull.

"Okay, you don't have to be sarcastic." The ball retriever licked his lips, staring into the eyes of one of the other patron's chests.

"I'm not being sarcastic, I just don't have much emotion when I talk sometimes." A soda spills across the room, and my adrenaline is crashing.

"Well you did earlier." In my defense, I had just committed arson at that point.

"Adrenaline crash, probably." The woman doesn't slap the machine or make anything of it.

"And what did you do to get adrenaline in the first place?" I miss another strike, didn't even make sense this time. It hit the first pin, then dove left, away from all of them.

Now if Phillus had told me this woman would be asking me what I did for fun, I probably still would've gone. I'm lonely. But that doesn't mean I want to tell this girl all about the crazy shit I do to feel alive. "Almost hit by a car this morning, really close. Went into fight or flight."

"Exciting, very glad you're not dead." She gives me a little wink before tossing the ball. It hits home, and so does the ball. Automatic strike, like a bowling machine. I bet if I asked her, she would probably say, "Oh yeah, I've bowled once or twice." She seems modest like that. It's not like I lied to her. I did almost get hit by a car. That car happened to lead me to a house.

The game ends swiftly, her beating me with a hundred and something to maybe ten. It's fun. She says next time she'll pick something I'm good at. That's a good sign that there will be a next time. Now I just need to find something I'm good at.

The restaurant across the street is, like I said, cucumber themed. It's an awful little dive, a huge, hulking pickle man standing on the roof, holding a plate of cucumber sandwiches. It's the closest place to the alleyway. I struggle, trying to pull open the door for my date, only to find it's a push door. Our waiter has, oh boy, a green apron and hat with little fake bumps on them. A smile and a wave and a few feet later we are sitting in a bumpy green booth. I am greeted with a menu, conveniently placed horror pickle on the front.

"So, Art, you didn't talk much about yourself on our last date either." She says this sipping delicately out of her brand-new water. Her bright lipstick smears where her glass leans against her lip.

"Yeah, I'm real lucky you talk so much, or else I'd be up a creek without a paddle." The waiter's pants are too tight.

"Yeah, you'd be in a real *sinch*. Well, are you any good at art, Art?" Her eyes are brown and lovely.

"I tried painting once. I tried painting coffee coasters." The waiter's shoes squeak, incessantly.

"What? Coffee coasters? Surely there's something more interesting than that you could have painted." Her hands are folded up below her chin now. It's time.

"Well, I can't say I wrung in gorgeous models, like the one in front of me back then. Coffee coasters are underappreciated anyway. You know, imagine me, sitting in my flat in California. Right here, sitting lotus style on my sucky fake fur carpet, and I'm holding a cup of coffee. Now I just bought this nice coffee table, and even though it's a coffee table, I don't want any stains on it. It was six hundred dollars, you understand?" She's a nodder. She doesn't hum in response to anything she hears.

"I certainly understand." She lies to spleet the ears of the groundlings.

"Good, good. Well, I'm sitting there, and I'm thinking to myself, geez, I wish I had a coasters—coaster, I mean, sorry. Now I get up and I look all over the house. This wasn't my house. I just happened to buy the table and pay the rent and live there, so I didn't really know where anything was. So I'm looking all over the place, and I check under the table. Now the neat thing about this table is, it had two little drawers, one of 'em empty and the other the perfect size for standard-size table coasters. Now I pull open the drawers, and lying inside is a single coaster, and it was the most beautiful coaster I've ever seen. I've summarized the search of the house for you, but I was looking for coasters for a good two hours. So this coaster was the most gorgeous creature I'd ever seen, I figured it needed a place in history forever." A plate falls in the kitchen facedown, and the entire kitchen staff is astonished it hadn't shattered.

"Now wait a second here, Art. If it took you two hours, wouldn't the coffee be cold?" She's sucking curiously at her glass and nodding occasionally. I've hooked her.

"Wonderful question, my dear. I've always taken my coffee cold. So I rush upstairs to this little gallery somebody set up, I paid for it, but I have no idea who set it up. Anyhow, it's this nice little painting studio, oil paints, acrylic, charcoal, anything you could need to paint the *Mona Lisa* except an old dead Italian. Now what I did was, I took the coffee coaster, and I leaned it up on a stool and put a little hat on it." I'm talking faster than a Nerdy White Kid on a very inexpensive skateboard, so about four miles an hour.

"Art! You're fooling with me, this is the most ridiculous story I've ever heard!" She laughs out loud, bouncing in her chair again.

"I promise you, every bit of it is true. Now I just had a big kick of inspiration, and this coffee coaster was posing so magnificently. I painted it in blues and yellows and gave the hat a deep black hue for contrast, it was a cream-colored beret, ya see. I would go on to buy more coasters for this home, and I painted every last one, all in different poses, all in different shapes. They decorated the walls of this home, from top to bottom." Somewhere out there, someone is malignantly eyeing a cucumber for different reasons than me.

"Well, what all happened to them, huh?" Her smile is coyish now, small and conniving.

I choke for a minute, trying to remember what happened to them. "Unfortunately, the house burnt to the ground, angry critics, you see."

"Oh, all right, Art. Jeez, you sure are a work of art." She says this as a confused and doldrum waiter snags his headphones on the chair behind us.

I haven't blushed in thirteen years, since this date I had with a girl that wore a shirt with a raccoon on it. She told me I had cute ears, and I didn't know what to do. However, this moment, with this girl probably five years too young for me, wrapped up in a story about a house I owned and burned down, and making a pun about my name, not even a good pun, this was the blush. The blush I've dreamed about since I was a schoolboy. The one that slashes your manhood and kills your pride and makes everything you'll ever want to do revolve around this person, like the sun to the earth, and even though it can kill you if you get too close, it is still the most gorgeous thing in the solar system. And all I can muster in response is "Thank you kindly."

Our food has arrived, and I am so incredibly ready. There is no surprise it had cucumbers on it, a little cucumber toothpick shoved in the top of my Reuben. She got a burger, and I fear she will find a garden of phallic vegetables inside. To my surprise, she comments on the lack of pickles.

"So listen, Art," she says between mouthfuls, "you keep saying you didn't own this house, that you clearly did."

"Well, no, that's very wrong." The pickle man atop the host's booth glares at me.

"Well, how is that?" I kick my heels together.

"Look at this restaurant here. Now imagine the owner. What will the owner do, say, if he decided his restaurant is disgusting and wants to tear the place down?"

"Well, he can't just do that!"

"Exactly! Who says he can't? He owns the place, right?"

"Well…yes, but that's different."

"Okay, here's another example. My house in California, it was built by a crew of construction workers. All the wood and stone and metal was flown in from China or Africa or someplace. Well, they build the house, and they fill the foundation with concrete, made in a mixer. That's not my mixer. I didn't build the place."

"Well…no, but you owned everything inside it."

"I didn't build a lick of furniture in that house. I bought the table, made in Thailand. I bought the hundreds of canvases from a local craft shop, who probably had them built by underpaid Asian children or something. All the other furniture, from Goodwill, not owned by me."

"Okay, well…you owned the imprint you left on it. The paintings! You certainly had to own those, it would be plagiarism if you didn't!" She's really heated with this debate.

"Incorrect. The paint was made from linseed and natural pigments, arranged in a fashion resembling hundreds of coffee coasters. The imprint I left on the house, maybe carbon and hydrogen and phosphorus residue. Carbon dioxide spewed from my lungs. None of it belongs to me, it was all fashioned fourteen billion years ago when one matter molecule decided to outweigh an antimatter molecule." The bird has taken the worm.

"So you're saying that no one has ever owned anything in their whole life."

"Now you're getting it!" I'm pink in the face. This exchange happens very quickly, and I say it all in about one breath. She takes maybe four or five, but I can tell the game has worn her down too. Conversation is like war, just different weapons.

She chews her last bite for a minute. Taking a pause to savor her cucumber water, still stained with that crimson hue, she replies, "Artemis…you surely are a strange fellow."

"In a good way or a bad way?"

"Maybe a little bit of both. I certainly want to see more, though."

This confrontation is rudely interrupted by our waiter, deciding it is appropriate to give us the check when neither of us are done. My tip will probably relate to manners, since he clearly needs some. Funny thing, though, the boy has a portable radio around with him. Strange that at lunch there were only a few customers, so I suppose he had time to listen to the news. "*Creature is very alive as it is presumed. The man is shoveling money to whoever asks about his prized pet. It is unknown how he obtained the reptile, but he appears to like showing it off. No one has been able to arrest him, on the account that he is very legally taking a crocodile for a walk. Be alert and wear closed toed shoes until the Friar leaves the city.*"

"Hannah, what might that radio be talking about?" She smiles confusedly, gazes toward the speakers in the ceiling, then to the hip of the waddling waiter, and wazammed out her vague recollection of its story.

"Oh yes! I heard about it this morning, an eccentric millionaire has brought his pet crocodile on vacation with him, visiting Portland today. I suppose it's a bucket list thing, he looked about ninety on the television." One of the kitchen doors slams angrily, followed by a language I've never heard.

"Well, let's go meet him!"

She laughs for a moment and then realizes I am serious. I've never seen a crocodile, and I would very much enjoy to. "Well, it would be one thing if we happened to bump into him, but I'd rather not go seek him out. He might have crocodile diseases or something."

"Now don't you be racist to crocodiles."

"I was referring to the man, but I apologize. I will watch my tongue when it comes to large reptiles."

"Not all of them, alligators are terrible. However, I've never met a crocodile, so I'm withholding judgement until I do. This might be one of my last opportunities."

"Well, I suppose we could take the tram downtown and look around." This line drags on as she is closing up her purse and grabbing her coat while saying it.

"Splendid!" I say that aloud as well as write it. I'm very happy she wants to accompany me. The hour is around 1:00 p.m., so I'd make sure to get her home at a decent hour. The train jostles, filled with all the people, not talking, just bobbing together at the same speed. This is what living in a city meant; the closer you are to people, the less you share with them. This whole train and here is this little bundle of joy next to me, the only bright soul in the whole car. Giving off enough light to make everyone else seem interesting.

"What do you do for fun, Hannah?" A clout of geese meets the reflection of her eyes through the window.

"I'm not really sure. I'm surprised that I'm as good a bowler as I am. Haven't done it since I was seventeen. I suppose I watch TV, and I do my hair in goofy styles and stuff like that. I used to have a turtle, hence why I want a tortoise so badly. The turtle was eaten. My roommate had a fight with me and happened to know many delicious turtle soup recipes."

"That's a terrible end for a pet."

"Well, it was either him or me. I ate it, was only natural. You know, the Aztecs used to eat their folks when they died. They did sacrifices and all that, but they were still the best astronomers and mathematicians in the new world." An old man with a pointy nose looks at me funny, thinking this is my daughter or something.

"Makes you think. Maybe they weren't wrong about all that, maybe that sort of brutality is normal." My flannel would have managed out a cry from the horrors it has witnessed.

"No, no, no, not at all like that. It was a sign of respect. Don't let their flesh go to waste. They honored their dead very well, built elaborate kingly tombs. They were different, crazy, and very, very interesting. Kind of like you." Her smile has faded, and now she is sitting, if possible, closer to me.

"What makes you think I'm a cannibal?" is all I can muster from the hundreds of privy eyes upon my lips.

"Not a cannibal. But you smell like chemicals and soot, and you have very interesting philosophy. You're an interesting man, and I like that. Perhaps not as much as the Aztecs, but you're also not dead, and you're not eating me, so that's a plus." She knew what she said. Her lips said it all.

I hold back a "That could be arranged," realizing she's the purest fruit in the history of decadence. "I'd say I'm a little better at English than the Aztecs as well."

"Maybe a *tad*." I fear she reads my mind, as us beastly men always do when our thoughts mingle with our groins, and a horrid display of sexuality is formed into words.

The rest of the ride is in silence till we got to the square. The square has a few police littered all over it. I don't much like police, but they do their job well here. They make sure that not a single homeless person gets to sit somewhere for more than ten minutes, those crazy folks. That's sarcasm, if you can't notice. There's some business with being behind certain lines and who can be where, but the homeless customs is a handbook to write at a different time.

She kind of skips off the train. It's strange that there's so many things that could make her a little girl. She's so freaking childish. Kinda scares me. Makes me feel like a creep, but that is immediately washed away by my quick mental analysis, realizing that, yes, I am a creep, and if ever there was a notion I am not a creep, then I might as well count myself dead. Maybe she has a weird past and has to act that way. Who knows, maybe I'll ask about it.

There's this neat little doughnut place by the square, kinda by my house. I go there every other day. The lady who works there is nice. She has a pointy nose that you can tell she's self-conscious about, but I don't know why anybody ever felt self-conscious about a big nose. By all means, it seems like a positive thing, more oxygen, originality, likeness to birds, more smells, etc.

"Hey there, Art, what'll it be today?" the chick says as I walk in. Shoot, I forgot I come in here every day.

"Well, I'll get a croissant and whatever this little lady might want," I say, gesturing to Hannah, who looks microscopic in comparison.

"I-I'll have a, uhhh, what's good here, Art?" she says, nudging me. I whisper "*anything*," and that isn't reassuring to her. "I'll get a, uhhh, a chocolate doughnut."

My cringe is noticed, and the woman laughs a little. She says, "The chocolate doughnuts are not his favorite, but I assure you, they're very good." It's because there was a fingernail in one of them once, and she swore to me it wasn't hers, and I swore to her that I will never again eat them.

Hannah chuckles a little and blushes, holding her hands at her hips. She looks very awkward, and I can't help but feel sorry for her. She talks a little with the woman. I think her name is Rebecca. I'll call her Rebecca. It suits her. I'm lying. I know that her name is Rebecca.

"So you know Art pretty well?" I manage to pick up. She really doesn't know me very well, but I think Hannah is a little intimidated. Rebecca is in every way my type, and I don't know why I hadn't pursued her. Maybe it's fate; Hannah has everything I need. The doughnuts are prepared with a tad bit of stubborn silence, and we leave. Or tried to leave. Hannah is very slow about it. It is in between the opening and closing of the door I realize we had abandoned the bill from cucumber hell.

There are more police around this time we leave, and I don't mind that. It just makes me paranoid. My opinion of Hannah keeps rising, and I am afraid she's noticed my paranoia. I've certainly noticed her paranoia, so it would be fair. I walk toward Chinatown, looking for a coffee shop on the way there I've been to. It doesn't matter which one I go to. She says something about the crocodile, but I can't hear her. I'm rushing. I'd like to think I'm not carrying her, but I might have been. I'm practically running. Anyhow, I find the shop, which ends up being a mile away, and I can't say she's quite happy with me by then.

"Artemis! What is wrong? I'm not much to run from, am I? I'm not in running shoes, please tell me what's wrong." There's also a pack of crows following us.

I mumble something about letting me sit down first, even though I'm already sitting. She sits in front of me, And her eyes look worriedly in my direction. Those big hazel eyes, the kind of eyes you'd remove glasses to see, the kind you could look at forever, are worried and tearing up for me. This is the time for me to tell her everything and the time for me to lose everything if she rejects me.

"I don't know what's wrong. You asked me what I do for fun, right? Please say yes." She nods, still a little confused. "Well, see, I don't do anything for fun. It's impossible for me to have fun. Phyllis called me the other day, to set up that date with you. That day, you were the first person who'd been interested in me for a long, long time. I had been an absolute scrooge for a few years, and I had to fix myself for you."

"I didn't know I meant that much to you alr—" The crow with the obnoxious overgrown egg horn perches on the windowsill.

"See, that's the thing. You do mean a lot, and that's why I'm going to tell you this next bit, and I want you to not tell me I'm crazy. Okay, good. See, I used to be a happy guy, but that was because I like destruction. I like ending things, I don't like seeing things be beautiful, and I'm very scared that that is going to happen with my relationship with you. I told you about that house I had in California, right? With all the coasters and the paintings and the designer suits and all the houseplants and my dog Stacey and even the goddamn unused barbecue that sat in the far corner of the patio always glaring at me. That one?"

By this point I'm yelling, and I'm yelling fast. I still haven't ordered anything, and I think that's drawn the attention of a few customers, but I don't care. "I burned it down. I set it on fire, I hated the whole thing. All of my possessions, all of everything I had created, it wasn't mine. I haven't owned a single thing in my life. This morning, I went on a walk over to the slums, and I found a door hanging wide open. Well, I was led there, but whatever. This house, it was just filthy. It smelled like chemicals and disgusting sweat and mildew. I walk around for a bit, and I see in the bedroom there's this couple lying on each other. Looks at first like they're sleeping, but I can tell different. The smell combined with the position, they were two meth heads that died right in the act, probably burst their hearts. It just made me so, so angry, that everything they had in the world was dying right there at the same time. I don't know how they died, and I don't care, but they were happy, and they were in love, and everything they ever owned was each other, and now that was gone, and I just couldn't have this paradise be seen by police. Sure, I'm romanticizing it a bit, but I don't want that to be us, you know? My first thought was these magnificent beasts need a proper cremation, so I took a Molotov in their fridge and burned the place down. My second thought was I need to be drunk, and then I needed to call you. Because you make me so, so happy, and I want nothing more than to die in a big, beautiful, disgusting house and just be one and then have some angel come and burn us down in a blaze of glory, I want to be with you, and I want to be in love and—"

I hadn't noticed she was screaming at me. She's calling my name. But I just keep talking. "I want us to be happy. I don't want to be some pyromaniac, I want to mean something to you. I want to mean something to me, I want to be more than those losers were. I know I just said that I want nothing more than that, but that's kinda just a thought. I called you in the middle of that burning house, and I don't want you to think I'm crazy, I just burn for you so much, and I want to be in love."

There is a silence. A silence you would have in a movie before a wild applause; however, this isn't a movie. This is a hole-in-the-wall coffee shop, where I'm just a freak that came in and started screaming. So I did what I thought would solve the issue. I go up to the counter, and I order a large iced coffee.

"Sir, I'm calling the police." This charmer should have been wearing a pickle hat.

"Not before you make my coffee. I came in here to talk to this wonderful woman and drink a coffee. I just did it out of order. For all you know, I'm an actor, and that was all an elaborate act. This is Portland after all, so relax and make my coffee."

The guy takes my four dollars and makes my coffee, and I go to sit back down across from Hannah. She's wide-eyed, can't even really cry. I know she wants to, and I don't want to stop her.

"Artemis...you...you're...I don't know what to say really. You're a psychopath if all that's true. I don't know what I'm supposed to think. What do you expect me to say?" Neither did the horny crow.

"Don't call the authorities." What a line.

"Okay...I won't call the police. Is that it? Do you expect our date to go back to normal? You were a little quirky, but now you're full-on insane!"

"I was always full-on insane. How is this any different?"

"Shit, I don't know, Art. My perception of you has changed, and though your...excuse is good, I don't know how I should feel. Are you telling me I caused you to burn down a house?"

"Not exactly, it was a spur-of-the-moment thing. It's not a serious crime, the house would have to be torn down anyhow, take it as vigilante justice, one year maximum. C'mon, please don't be afraid or anything."

"You just confessed a lot of crazy things, and your view of someone you've only known for about eighteen hours. I really like you too, but I just can't get over your perception of me. How can you just...think like that?"

"I think a little differently, I'm sorry. I've never had anyone I've loved before, and I've concluded that it's you."

She stares for a little bit. I get my coffee, and I sit back down. A sip or seven later, she's talking a little again. "It's crazy...I suppose I'm a little crazy too. I can't say I reciprocate, but I do think I can help you and care for you. You don't seem…murderous, but I'm still scared to get to know you."

"You don't have to get to know me then!" I say this while making eye contact with an old woman whose head is shaped like a clam, one of the ones that they keep in Asian food stores that stick out that tube-tongue thing that's three times the length of the shell. That's her head. She sits a few seats behind Hannah and has no relevance to the story besides that she's there.

"Damn it! That's what a relationship is, knowing and trusting each other." The sigh that comes out is elaborate and exaggerated. She wants it to be part of what I hear. She wants me to hear her sigh and take whatever her breath passes out as truth, but I can't hear anything but a sigh. "I guess we can agree to a third date then?"

"Absolutely, I'd love to." The crow has long since flown off, and I hadn't noticed it leave.

"I know you would but…give me your number so I can decide when. I don't know if I really want to see you right now."

And that's how the date ends, watching that purple suit-dress bounce away, attached to its very conflicted owner. I decide to tip the bistro four dollars and walk home. I always liked the number 8. I go over the conversation over and over in my head, thinking about how it could have ended so much more peacefully. If only I wasn't such a lunatic!

I don't know I'm crying until I notice the wetness on my mouth. I thought I was bleeding. It's been so long since I've cried. I can't remember the last time it happened. I honestly looked like a mess. My hair hasn't been kept since 2005, and I look like a stroke victim, never showing emotion. But this is emotion, one I haven't had for an extended amount of time.

You see all these people on the street here, living without homes. Living and doing drugs, paying attention to nothing but substance. Why do we judge that? When you live a life where no one wants you, you have no home, nothing to read, maybe no education, what else is there? There's no way to get rid of your diseases, so why fear them? Dive deeper, I say. If I could afford to buy these guys any drug of their choice, I would, but right now I'm a shitty online critic. Getting paid to hate things. I'm good at what I do. Look me up, Artemis Desantos, I'm the most horrible critic anyone can listen to, but I get paid by the review, and I can review just about everything.

My dreams are weird that night. There's this one person who always appears in my dreams. I call him the Bomber, because he makes bombs out of weird things. He's got a weird habit of saying nothing ever. He's always at this long table with a microscope and this telescoping welding machine. Last time I checked in on him, he was making bombs out of sugar crystals, placing each grain of sugar over a grain of TNT, patterned. He ended it by making it look like a sugar cube by spraying it lightly with heat. He explained without talking that when it drops into a mug of liquid, it'll blow up and pierce whoever's holding it with glass. But tonight he's unusual.

Tonight the Bomber is taking Hannah apart. It's simple, that's what he was doing. There she is, lying on the table in what is soon to become pieces. Of course it isn't grotesque. I've never had gore in any dream I've ever had, but I see her bones and rib cage and that beautiful smiling face so confused and pure in comparison to the surgical exposure. She's still functional. I watch him use the tool to pry her ribs open, one by one and pull out her heart. He makes sure to clip the tubes and hold it pumping in his hands. She gasps and seizes, her lungs pulling in and out hard, and it looks like she's trying to talk. But she can't breathe. There's steam pumping out of her veins. Her hazel eyes are becoming bronze. And then to a shiny, metallic tin. This color moves down her body, her face is aluminum and then her neck, then each of her ribs. In a minute, her whole body is a shiny chrome, and she breathes deeply. The bomber holds the heart in his hand, cauterizing the veins with a cigarette lighter and keeping the thing beating. He stares at it under a microscope. I can't help but try to wake her from her trance. I say, "What are you doing, wake up, you're clearly alive. Get your heart! You need that!" But she won't listen. She just presses a cold metal finger against my lips. The bomber pours power into her heart, then a liquid, and then stitches it up. He holds his trophy as it continues beating. He wipes off his scalpel and stands, something I've never seen him do before, and he hands it to me. He says, "It's your choice, it still works. It was more damaged before I touched it." I hold the small organ instinctually to my breast and feel it tense and retract. In tune with the ticking of my own empty metal heart, I couldn't have them so close together.

What did I do? I put it back inside of her. Her skin is growing back as metal. All of her is covered, and I have to pry open her metal rib cage. My fingernails rip off, my hands are bloody, and I keep pulling. My hands are cut by her sharp edges. After rip and tear and metal regeneration, finally, I put her heart back where it belongs. Her body forms around it and stays that same shade of chrome but smoothed out. She grins and tells me something in Enochian. However, then the ticking began. *Tick, tick, tick.* Then, a sudden thud and metal bits and clockwork gears fall everywhere over the room. And I'm woken by the telephone.

I don't answer it. It's 4:00 a.m., and I don't want to answer it. I can't handle talking, and I can't handle reality after that. Not that I'm traumatized, I just hate the thought I created. Here I was, this freak my brain gave birth to, giving me love advice. That's ridiculous. Then the answering machine turns on. It's from Hannah, and I not listening until half of her message is over. It's unreal that she would call me tonight.

"*So* unhappy. That's how it's always been. I honestly thought you'd hate me, think I'm too giggly or childish or anything like that. I know you're, what, three or four years older than me, but I guess that's why I like you. You seem like you can keep it in check. Of course, now I don't but I'd say I'm just as crazy. I don't really trust you, but who really trusts anyone these days. I don't trust myself, I don't trust you, nobody in that damn restaurant trusts us after you told that guy to get a real job! That was just so immature but so funny. I guess that's what I want, someone to be happy with whether I trust them or not. I mean…maybe you're pissed I kinda rejected you like—love me. I hate that word, you know? I kinda wish you hadn't have used it. But that's not the point. I accept you, and well, I can't sleep, so I figured if you wanted to talk. But you probably won't listen to this because you think I hate you so. Good morning, I guess. Peace."

She's disappointed I don't answer her. I have an ultimatum here. I can call her back or I can go back to bed and pretend I didn't hear anything she said. It comes to me that if I leave her alone, she will destroy herself. So I decide I would invade her home uninvited, because I've already spat on every piece of self-respect I had, so why not my respect for her boundaries?

It's a cold morning, and the streets are fresh with early morning commuters. No pedestrians yet but lots of people coming down from every other city in the world, to sit in a tall building and type things. It's a horrible way to live, and I'm proud to participate.

Before I enter that tall, tall building at the edge of downtown, I could have sworn I saw an old man with a cane followed by the tail of a reptile from the corner of my eye. Maybe it's what I wanted to see. But it's a reason to talk to her. The inside of her complex is cold too. Perhaps they don't have a thermostat.

There were so many things I feared that could go wrong. I was positive the elevator would smash to the bottom floor and the force of it would crush my bones instantly. I was certain my chances of being confronted by Mr. Jackson would increase, and worst of all, I was afraid of rejection. Here I was, staring at that gross green door that opened up to her living quarters. Then, there I was, saying "knock" and knocking again. Kill your pride, Artemis, this is your bottom of the barrel.

She opens the door and asks who it is while opening it, a redundant action, but I like it anyway. "Oh…Art. I was really hoping I didn't hope it was you. But I did, and I'm not going to ask you why you're here. Just come in." She looks a lot different with smeared makeup and baggier clothes. Looks more like me, less of an idol.

She isn't chipper. She isn't giggly. She isn't stoic like she sounded in the message. She looks broke. Her makeup is leaking with tears that dribbled down to an oversize pink robe, faded pink like the color of a diseased flamingo. Her aura seems down and low, like someone had broken her spirit. Her apartment isn't in good shape either. I expected some kind of pristine home with flowers everywhere and pretty tapestries. She lives plainly, computer and junk, other chords in the corner next to her bed. A small table and chairs and a kitchenette with built-up dishes. Her clothes lay in a basket in the corner of her room, and cans litter the floor. A fairly normal bedroom, but nothing more than that. However, all over the walls hang a bunch of drawings. All weird drawings, of surreal worlds and strange planets and inhuman creatures. It's wonderful.

"Here's my home…I hope you enjoy it. I didn't bother fixing it up because I expected a phone call, but whatever. Are you all right?"

I really dig that, that she's worried if I'm all right. "I'm perfect, only because you asked that."

"You realize how unrealistic this is," her downtrodden lips mumble.

"Yes, I'm awaiting Samuel L. Jackson any minute."

"What?"

"Oh Jesus, don't say that, you'll summon him."

What comes after is a defeated cry, what the great vampire slayer Abraham Van Helsing called King Laugh. A kind of boiling point, the teakettle boiling over and screaming for you to use it. Her voice is still hoarse from a flood having left her eyes, and her breath is taut, but it is a laugh. The kind of laugh you get from someone who heard the last joke in their life, the kind of laugh you hear in thick static, the kind of laugh that makes you think this person has a past but they don't have a future so here they are living in the present, and the present happens to be something they don't want to find funny but do. I might be romanticizing it, but that laugh broke my heart. It broke her heart, and it made me decide I want to fix it. "Leave it to Artemis to make a pulp fiction reference when you're trying to have an emotional conversation."

"I'm trying to cheer you up. I know it's unrealistic for me to get the girl at the end. I figure it won't happen, and that's because I don't want to get you. I want you to understand me and me to understand you and have us melted together in some abomination of broken thoughts and feelings. I don't know why you hurt, and it doesn't matter why you hurt because no matter what, I'm going to fix it."

She chokes, sobs without saying anything. She sits on the bed and slumps over. I take my seat at those cheap ass chairs and just let her. I don't try to soothe her because I know she won't listen. This is her belly of the whale and my crossing the threshold. Guess I just got lucky on who the hero here is. Her tan frame, slumped over, wetting her mattress with tears, and I'm certain she deserves happiness but also certain she deserves sadness. One cannot play the play of life without all the characters. The villain is no less or more vital than the court jester, and it's funny we think of sadness as bad, but by god, it makes you feel more alive than any other emotion on the planet. It's that chemical that makes you want to tear everything to pieces and makes you want things you don't have more than ever. It's a puddle that sits in your brain and invites you to swim, but when you do, the water is so much colder than you expected, so you just wade along and wait for it to get warmer, but it never does. You just shiver and cry and feel how badly you want that warmth until you realize it isn't going to be in this pool, so you get out and find another. That's probably what she's going through, floating on this freezing mattress in the middle of an ocean, and the only thing there to comfort her is this burning man that wants to heat up her world but can't. The burning man that dances tiptoed over the water, pretending he doesn't notice the little tip of his blazing toe getting chillier with every step, because now he has a project to use his heat for, as long as he dances in step.

That's why I stayed. I stayed because I hoped I could help her. I hoped this was real and she was real and the pouring 5:00 a.m. rain outside was real and that we could both just exist in each other and not be two distant beings drowning with the capability to breathe for the other. The bird of paradise and the fiery phoenix, here they were, and here they would stay, never mixing but never separating. I like to think of it like that.

"It's not real, Art," the wind says, as if her voice were just a sad gust.

"I was going to say the same thing, doll." Her room smells like oil paint and roses.

"I'm no doll." The clouds are now dry; they only threatened lightning.

"Yes, you are, look how small and pretty you are."

"That's not what I mean. I'm not some plaything." She is the storm.

"No, you're not that kind of doll. You're a little Victorian-era porcelain doll, when they used real lipstick and real hair so that it would look so very close to human, but shying off because of those gorgeous, strange-colored eyes. You're the kind that someone finds in an antique store, and they see it and think it's the most beautiful thing, and they'll pay no matter what price they offer, because you're goddamn worth it. You're the kind of doll that's been sitting and collecting dust for far too long. You need someone to treasure you."

"You have a way with words." I've been struck.

"I've spent a lot of time talking to myself, and I don't listen to boring people." I'm burning up.

She gets up, and I couldn't help but compare our statures. I'm sitting straight up on the chair, and she's head height with me. She can't have been more than five feet, and it's wonderful. She leans her head on my shoulder, and I pat her silky curly locks. Not as soft as I'd imagined, but I think I like it better that way. I don't tell her everything is going to be all right. I know nothing is going to be all right. I know this night is the most impossible thing that could have ever happened.

"I saw the crocodile man before I came here."

"What?"

"Hush that. I saw the old guy pulling the crocodile around just by your apartment. Maybe he's still out there, check the window." And so she does. She has this kind of fire escape outside her window, and she climbs onto it, looking down at the world, ninety feet down. She doesn't really look for anything. I think she wanted an excuse to go outside. It was probably good for her.

"Art, how many stories does it take to guarantee death?"

"None, because I'm not letting you jump."

"Dang."

I stand next to her for a while, the cold morning breeze ruffling our hair and making our lungs fill with a hundred people's breaths. A hundred other sighs, a hundred other screams, and here they were being recycled and brought into us.

"Worst-case scenario, you reject me."

"Artemis, I can't reject you, I'm already dependent on you, and it's only been about a full day."

"You can still reject me. Doesn't matter how long we're together, I can still be rejected."

"What makes you say that?" The sun is rising.

"Haven't had a relationship go well, ever. No big sob story, just impossible to live with."

"Double for me." Far too early.

"Why?"

"I'm a slob, I'm too childish, and I have too many bad memories." And still, out there over the city, it is orange and yellow.

"Now name the bad qualities."

"Those are them. Do you expect me to tell you my life story?" Slowly.

"Not really, I don't think it's important. What's important is now."

"Rude." But surely.

"But true."

"Get out, stop making sense, you big killjoy." That big ol' circle peeks its head out of the clouds.

I want so badly to hold her hand. I haven't wanted to hold someone's hand since I was fifteen, and it's a wonderful feeling. It seems unreal, and I don't want it to end by trying to. It's like the desire would be a better feeling than the goal. So I decide to avoid it. I just stand with her, content in my ignorance and content with my emotions and just content.

"I could deal with this every day." I really could too. I really wanted to. This small woman was now everything I held dear. Considering sirens came from the direction of my home, maybe, just maybe I'd have to get lost and go somewhere.

"I know you could, you've told me a few hundred times."

"I don't think I need to set any more fires."

"I think you do. I sure can't set fires."

"Really? Well I'll be your fire if you be my kindling."

"Sounds like a deal."

I really don't like happy endings. I really abhor them, simply because they never happen to me. This isn't really a happy ending, but more of a happy...middle. Not a beginning for either of us, but here we are, meeting in the middle with cops cars blazing down the street and a beautiful urban sunrise watching two sad people learn to be sad with each other. It sounds romantic, but it's really just a cool thing to say before killing somebody. Say "what" again, I dare you.

GIVING UP

I can feel it on my neck, hatred. Everywhere, all around me just floating there, waiting for me to take notice. It's in the paint, I swear. I'm just waiting, hoping, knowing that she'll be back soon. She was just here yesterday. People hate me when she's not around. Everyone loves me when she is. She isn't here, and I'm scared.

"Cain, how are you? Are you okay?" she says. It makes me happy, ecstatic. I learned so many things I want to tell her. I learned a lot from the *National Geographic*s I've been reading. Like those crazy blue holes down in Indonesia where there's more liquid hydrogen than there is water. Got some crazy critters living down there. They have this kind of shrimp that doesn't ever touch the cave walls. It just swims around like a fish its whole life. I want to tell her about that, but she isn't here.

I sit all day in this little room, the nurses and their doctors and all their patients are always going about. I'm not sick, I like watching them scuttle around now. Every now and then, Terry will tell me bad things. That's not all the time. Only sometimes. Terry is my puppet, the one with the eyes, the misshapen ones. One of them is yellow, and the other is red. They're both buttons, but I like to pretend their eyes. I made Terry, and now he can talk to me.

"She's never coming back. You know she isn't, she has no reason to." Terry will scream around me. He thinks she's a traitor, that she doesn't deserve our approval. He hates her, and I have to listen sometimes. He's the one who speaks when she's here.

"I hate you! You're a miserable child, and I want nothing to do with you!" I see him scream. He tells me it's better than letting her in. She'd only hurt us. She's a horrible person, obviously. He makes her mascara run, that pretty makeup she wastes so much time on. I want to hug her and tell her he doesn't mean it.

"Cain, you need to calm down. You know I have to go away for a while…do you promise you'll be good?" she mumbles back. She's too nice to Terry, far too nice. I used to be so smart, how come Terry won't let me talk? The walls are yellow today.

"No! I don't need to calm down, you just need to leave! I won't have your deceit and your wasted breath. Get out!" He keeps using my mouth to make pain. Why?

Her dainty hand reaches out, and she caresses the puppet. She's crying, why is she crying? Her face is pointed down, and she just holds Terry and bawls. I can't hug her, I can't do anything to help, so my weary eyes just watch her. Watch her cry, wanting her to know I want her here, but I can't show any emotion. The analog clock keeps ticking, in old black-and-white movies with the actress only history remembers, and no one remembers that anyhow.

Sometimes I want her here. The other people aren't very nice. They're always blaming me for things. I had to cook things last week. I had to cook a turkey dinner. It was turkey day! I had to cut up the onions. I had to dice them and make them look pretty and then put them in the stuffing. I had to make a lot of stuffing. We have a lot of friends here. But I couldn't cut the onions very well. I tried to cut them, and I got scared. I got scared my hand would move on its own. I didn't want my hand to disobey me, so I threw the knife, and it landed on someone's shoes. I tried to tell them I didn't mean to, and they said it's okay, but I know they're lying. I know that they want to get me back, and when I turn around, I'm going to get it. I can't be in the kitchen anymore.

They stopped giving me medicine. The woman told them that it won't help. I know it will help, but she won't try it out. She just wants me to die in here. She wants them to starve me. I used to have a nice car. I used to drive it everywhere, all around the big city. I can't remember where I took it. I know she sold it! There's no way she couldn't have. If I had that big car, I would leave here.

What did I used to read? I read the Harry Potter books, that's what I remember. I never understood why Voldemort didn't like Harry's dad. I think that Ron was too annoying, always asking for help when he could've just thought about it. I don't remember much besides that. I know that at the end, Harry and Voldemort die, I think. There can't be two of them, and one couldn't live without the other. I used to read a lot. I used to read to that girl, the one that sees me all the time. I used to read all sorts of things to her. I read most of those Harry Potter books out loud to her. I remember she was so happy then, so small. So carefree.

"Cain, what day is it?" The white walls behind the doctor wink at me.

"December thirteenth, sir," I say to them, angrily if I could muster it.

"How old are you, Cain?" They're throwing up gang symbols now.

"I'm a good age, sir." I can't let them watch this spiral.

"How many years have you been alive, Cain?" The doctor turns around, and they stop doing what they were doing.

"Forty-six years, sir." I try to remember how many years there had been in each of those forty-six years, but I can't.

"What do you remember about the past few years, Cain?" He touches his beard like it's in any way important.

"I remember that I've been here. I haven't been doing much, I read the *National Geographic*, and I eat my meals, and I don't bother anybody. I don't mean to bother anybody, please don't let them say I'm bothering anybody." I'm bothering everyone. The walls are bleeding from all the discomfort of my voice.

"Cain, you don't need to get scared. You're safe, you're not bothering me. Who told you that you bothered them?" I can't read his teeth. He doesn't have any.

"Well, Terry knows I'm bothering everyone. He keeps me shut up so I don't start anything funny." A crow is pecking at the window, like a woodpecker of the sorrows we produce.

"Who's Terry?" I hate this person. He always asks these kinds of questions. He knows who Terry is. I see him all the time. He wants to make sure I'm in the same mood. I always have to think about his questions. He never asks me anything nice. He never asks me what I read recently or asks what I saw on television. He never asks.

"When will that lady be back?" *He means Amy,* Terry corrects for me.

"Amy will be back tomorrow. You need to wait. Who's Terry? Who was Terry?" *An old man in a Chinese lamp shop, what the fucks it matter to you?*

"You know." No, I am not allowed to know.

"No, I don't know. When did you meet Terry?" He speaks too slow. It makes my ears sigh and wail.

"I DON'T WANT TO TALK ANYMORE!" I didn't mean to scream. They used to let me talk in his office, but he made me angry a lot. I had to make that nice lady replace a lot of his things. He's always mean to me, though. I threw his table once, and another time I threw his coffeepot. I think he still has the pieces. Maybe I'll fix it for him to apologize.

"We still have twenty-eight minutes. What would you be willing to talk about?" *He's thinking for his peers, who want nothing to do with you for the rest of this session. He's a martyr, Cain.*

"Tell me about the ocean, mister." He's not very old. He has a big beard, but it's a young guy's beard. I don't have facial hair anymore. They cut it off for me. I know plenty about the ocean. I knew a little guy there. He owned a boat. I'd go down to the boat dock, and we would fish all the time. That was long, long ago, when I was the same age as this guy in front of me.

"What do you want to know? I can't say I doctored in oceanology!" He smiles big and bushy, like he said something real funny.

"How are the seagulls right now?" Down on the waterfront, shitting on the tourists that make the most noise.

"Well, you can look outside. They come down here in the winter, remember?" It is December, I forget.

"I used to make snowballs too, we'd go take snowballs and throw 'em. And she always said that she wanted to make a snowman, but

I didn't know how to make a snowman! So what I did, I built a fort for her, out of snow that was already there. The funny thing is when the fort was built, it turned out to be a car covered in snow, and we couldn't do anything with it. She was always asking me questions. I used to know the answers…" *Shut up.*

"Who are you talking about, Cain?" *The vampire, who else would I be talking about?*

"I don't know, that woman that comes in here. The one Terry doesn't like."

"Are you going to be nice to her?" He looks worried now, worried like I'm going to hurt him or something. *Him.*

"I'm always nice to her. Terry isn't nice to her. Terry is better than me, so it's hard to control him." *It's pecking.*

"Why doesn't Terry like her?" *Peck.*

"Because he just doesn't. He is trying to protect me." *Peck.*

"Why will he protect you? Look at Terry. Terry is a puppet. Who was Terry before he was a puppet?" *Pecking at the mask.*

I don't like these questions. They're long and boring and make me sick. I just want to go home and look at pictures of flowers. I used to like flowers. I had to be a mama for a while. I had to learn how to do all those things. I had to learn cooking and flowers and all those things little girls like. I'm not a real man anymore. People think that all the time. I don't care, as long as I'm quiet, and I don't disturb anyone.

"I'm trying to break you from these delusions. You used to be curious. You used to say, Dr. Conner, please explain to me what's happening with my head. Cain, I can help you, I did help you, just open up. Please. Who was Terrance?" Dr. Conner isn't being very professional.

"He's just a puppet…"

"Say that again? I don't think that's right." He's desperate.

"He's a puppet that talks, that's all he is."

"I've never heard him talk! I heard Terry talk, and you did, so tell me who was Terry?"

"Terrance Ray died on November 30, 2005." I didn't say that. Terry said that. He wrote it down a long time ago, and I read it. He left these journals in my cupboard. *Idiot mixed up the names.*

"Good. Who was Terrance Ray?"

"Terrance Ray was a sailor."

"Yes. Whose brother was he?"

"Me and Kelly's." *Dumb whore.*

"Who was Kelly? What did Terrence do?" *Okay, well, that's my business, Doc.*

I can't remember the movie. I can't remember the book. I can't remember anything, and I feel so ashamed. I don't know why I feel that way.

"Doc Conner...can I please go home? I don't want to be here." My face is heavy.

He sighs. He doesn't breathe very heavy, but here he is, sighing. He says I can go. I'll have to look through more of that writing. I like it. Whoever wrote it was very smart. I keep it in a cupboard in my room. They don't have locks on it anymore. I had to promise them I wouldn't stab myself with the pens. They keep saying they'll get me a typewriter, but they never do. They've been saying that they'll do that for lots of years now. They tell me they'll do something but don't. It's annoying.

This guy wrote a lot of nice things. Here's the first thing he wrote. "The lights are fading recently. I fear I'll have to call the technician. I used to aide this hospital, funny. Now here I am, a patient. I suppose I accept it, though. I'd rather raise Amy from here than raise her in that godforsaken house. I'm not really sure what to write about, but I have to get my thoughts out before they're gone. I'm thirty-nine years old. My name is Cain Ray. I have a ten-year-old daughter named Amy, and I killed my brother on the thirtieth of November last year. I do not know what happened, my mind left me, and I was certain he was an enemy. I've been on edge since then. I pleaded insanity, and now here I am. Thankfully, my wit is still here, and I'm on good terms with most of the doctors. There's one, a young fellow, my psychiatrist. He's been giving me medication to go with my severe paranoid schizophrenia, or so they decided I have.

I've talked to him about sailing. I've sailed, sailed to Australia from Florida. An awfully long journey for two men. Terry went with me. He didn't much enjoy having me on the boat. Dr. Conner is very interested in sailing. He asked me what kind of birds I saw. There were a few on the open sea, but only migrating seagulls. There's lots of fish, however, and I made sure to catch lots of fish. I've shown him pictures, saw a lot of seabass. He's a nice guy. It's ironic, I have no reason to be here, but yet, I am. I used to have so much inspiration. Now all I have is white walls and paper cups. Nothing to keep me happy, but it's this or prison."

He sounds like a nice guy. They want me to get rid of it. All his writing. They say it's bad for my head, that the medication was harming me and that's why I wrote those things. I wasn't the same me I am now. I am a conundrum, they say. Who are they? Why are they? Who is deciding that I am being governed by something unnatural, by some magical group of people that know all and see all and, more importantly, decide all? I decided long ago that in my moments of clarity, such as this one, I would hate everything with all my being. I know that they are talking about me, talking about my delusions, my pitiful appearance, the persona I have to cover myself. These are the moments when I write, and the me I am usually will read it and love it, and perhaps I can break through. Amy hasn't come in for several weeks. I think she's distracted, probably with a boy or a girl or whatever the hell she's into these days. I don't bother. I don't bother with anything. I won't bother with anything. I used to bother. I used to yell and scream and get angry about my imprisonment. I am Cain Ray, Amy Gladys Ray is my daughter, and she refuses to tell me that she hates me. She hates my being. She hates the home I killed her uncle in. She thinks I left it to her as a punishment. One day, she'll stop getting checks. She'll have to get a job, and she'll curse me for coddling her so. She'll curse me for leaving and hate me with all her being. All that takes place now in the rare moment of thought, the rare moment of understanding everything, the times I have to take in everything that is and will be and spit it out onto paper so the dribbling fool that can't even remember his own name can read it and giggle. I hate him. He calls me Terry. I killed my brother for a reason, and now ironically I am labeled as him for the entirety of our lives. One day, very soon, I will decide to die. I am already dead, in this instant, and the doctors are reading what I'm writing as I'm writing it and at the same time reading it an hour after I've been pronounced dead, and their curious scientific minds will finally grasp that which they badgered around for the past seven years I've been here. In these moments, the moments where I can pretend I'm more than a ghost strapped to a melting psyche, is the moment outside of time. Time doesn't exist to me anymore. I am aware that in a few moments, the nurse will come in and ask me if I'd like my medicine, and I'm going to tell her no, because in that instance, I will not be who I am now. I will be the fool that calls me Terry, and that fool is convinced medicine keeps me alive. Which it does, and that is why he refuses to take it. The ego has killed the ego and split itself in two to become a horrible monstrosity. All my mercy, all my joy, and all my stupid self-acceptance, all my paranoia and all duress has been packaged into a stupid person that lives on the outside, shielding my timeless mind on the inside. I don't like the word *self-contradictory*. It bothers me because it's too true.

I had a scary dream again last night. It was the same one as always with the little girl and the man who looks like me. I don't like that man, but I know a lot about him. He always looks up at me and smiles before he starts. His teeth are yellow and pointed and gross. I feel like he'll come get me one of these days. He should brush more. Then the little girl walks in. The man smiles down at her with such happiness, so joyful. He has wanted to see her all day. She hops onto his lap and lays into his belly and says something I can't hear. He says something back, but they're words I don't understand. His teeth are sharp again, his eyes bleeding, and he screams. He screams, scratching his jagged arms across the girl. She won't stop bleeding, and she is screaming for dad. She wants her dad to make him go away, but he says that it is for her safety, that bleeding will make her human. She's such a cute little girl. He only wants to save her, in his sick, twisted sense. He's never been a bad man. He just trusted too much in Mama. But he is now, and that is unforgivable. He ruined it. He ruined everything I could possibly be happy about. The simpleton and the sailor and my own damn twin brother, and he had to snap first. I can't stand seeing how he convinces her so easily that she's inhuman. She's just a little girl! You have it all wrong. There is nothing wrong with her! Only you! He is standing now, and I can see the scars all over her, all over her from the times he's tried to humanize her. She hardly sheds a tear anymore, and I let it happen under my nose. Asking him to fucking babysit!

"I'm so sorry for this, Amy," I whisper in my sleep. Was it a dream? Or was it just an old memory under the bed? They don't let me keep anything under the bed anymore. Afraid I'll hurt myself with it. You can't hurt yourself with a memory.

"Have you ever been a religious man, Cain? You know, my father-in-law is a priest. Do you think being in touch with your maker would help shake you from this delusion?" Conner says, holding a Bible on his side.

"All I know 'bout is my cursed name."

"How is it cursed? I didn't know you knew anything from the Bible." He's lying to me. We've talked about it before.

"Son of Adam, forced to be immortal when all he wishes is to die." I don't know what the one with *I* means, but it sounds right.

"But you aren't immortal. You will pass away when the time comes, like every man does," he assures me. He knows what I mean.

I don't say anything for a long, long time. I just stare at the clock. Stare at him. Stare at the wall and the air floating in between our heads. "There's an awful lot to think about when you have no family left."

Dr. Conner tried to show no emotion. He was a young doctor when I met him. He wore pressed suits and made sure to look professional before he found his style. His style is indifference. He drops religion because both of us are agnostic. I know he knows me. He knows this is all an act. But this moment is real weakness. From both parties, there is emotion.

"Dr. Conner. Do you think Terry forgives me?" *I can see an inkling of a tear.*

"I don't think he's worthy of forgiveness, Mr. Ray. In my opinion, it should be him in here and not you." He pushes up his glasses and straightens the papers in awkwardness.

"That's the part you don't get, Doc. We were both crazy. It's one thing to kill a brother. But to kill a twin? There's something wrong there, a real lunacy. Amy would have been better off with her mother. Look at her now! Off with some lowlife that can't fucking sleep. Do you call that life, Doc? Do you think that my murder was worth that? I could have talked to him, I could have made him get the help he needed." He tried to interrupt me. I wouldn't let him. "Amy is a strong girl. I have a lot of time to think, and if…if I explained what was wrong, nothing would have had to happen. I shouldn't have let emotion have its way." And there I am now, holding his neck between my hands, squeezing and yelling while she watches, licking her wounds and curled in a ball while her daddy kills the other daddy, the one that told her she wasn't worth life unless he treated her, the stupid one that couldn't even think well enough to control his head. The one that was too dumb to understand that there was no such thing as blood-thiefers, and I'm squeezing every bit of life out of him. Like killing a baby for putting a stain on the couch.

"It's all forgotten in the end. When something ends, that should be it. Keep picking at it and you'll make it worse." *Peck.*

"We're both doctors, sir. You and I both know that we're immortal. All of my sins, all of your sins, will be carried for eternity with our names. Don't tell me I'm innocent. Don't you dare tell me you're innocent. Forgiving and forgetting is well and fine for the blame dodgers out there, but I'm not one of them. Do you remember my article about time and space and where consciousness fits into the whole thing?"

"Yes, I do, Cain. I remember you read it to me very well and told me how you would love to someday meet who wrote it." A smile of assurance meets his face, and I see he thinks I've broken.

"I've met who wrote it, and it isn't either of us. It's the burning soul out there who's just looking for love. They wrote the whole damn thing, and we're all that soul. I'm so goddamn nuts, Doc. I've been stuck in a horrid shell for so long, and god knows how I got so broken in the head. I can't do a damn thing I ever could, and why is that? Why must I turn on myself, in complete faith of myself. It's a joke, told by a fucking eunuch with cerebral palsy trying to utter the words to the punchline, but people can't stop laughing at him hitting himself in the nonexistent balls. I'm so tired, Doc. Just tell me a story."

"Whatever will make you feel better."

I plan on dying tonight. That's been decided several hundred tonights ago. But the good doctor here will give me something to help me out, because I get to choose the story, and I know how to pull his strings. I'm going out on my own terms. Have fun in hell.

ASSUMING WE WERE
SOLIDS TO BEGIN WITH

As it did when he was a boy, the cold Willamette air made his nose tingle. As it always had, the trash and refuse that littered the street filled him with disdain for his human peers, but he snipped that thought in the bud after looking at what flowed in his veins and what flowed out of them and why the *H* word no longer applied to him.

The old man was in the ruined square, that lovely little four blocks of space that once held hundreds of tourists at a time. He'd seen it when it was just trees. He'd seen it when this city hadn't hardly sprouted and folks called it Stumptown.

The bridge where the boy had his first kiss was still bleeding with dew and would forever in the absence of the dewdroppers. Somewhere down there was the river.

In the buildings, the blackened victims of the fall watched and calculated where the traveler's footsteps would lead, but only in the time of night could they act. He smelled different than most folks that came through.

Memories bothered him. Faces he remembered that were now ash. The woman who left him here, the man who left him there, the couple that laughed at him there. All gone, while he, the outcast, was left alive, to spit on the remains of his comrades. Youth, long ago destroyed, was replaced only with pain. Only with absence. He scratched his scarred face and recalled what it was like back when he last saw this place.

The old man stood in the half circle of bricks and looked. Here, you could not hear yourself speak. Or perhaps you could hear everything speak. It no longer worked, and so it didn't matter.

The clouds always appeared like they would rain but never did. Constant gloom overhung the city, and the deadfellas loved it. O'Brien placed binoculars before his mismatched eyes. One was metal, to see later, and one rotting, to see before, both inky green. His blackened teeth knocked out. "Boys, we've another down the road."

"What's its shape this time?" the others chattered, half loony.

"Man again. Midlife it seems. It's not there tomorrow."

"May as well send a—" Before the poor flunky could utter his speech, a rock came and filled its mouth, breaking what remaining teeth it had. That rock was delivered by the now-charging stranger toward the building these fellows stayed in, formerly referred to as the Big Pink.

It took a minute for the cognition to return to O'Brien; the dusty, cobweb-ridden memory recess of his mind to spin, and he recalled the face of the stranger, from somewhere back in the living world, but couldn't place a name.

The waterfront was cold and without water. Looking down off those cliffs, at how much water there once was, was enough to sadden the old man. The constant empty holes which would fill to suppress flooding were no longer needed, and falcons screeched from their graves. He asked why he had been unable to see this, why all this, which could have been easily prevented, was the only thing he could not change. Why the air, which spun to his beat, was now so harsh and biting at his heartless skin. He saw, down in the dust, fifty-some feet down, a smile from a head with no body, and he sighed, sighed at this silliness.

"Where is the news! What are you doing wasting your life, man?" asked the traveler, sitting with O'Brien's binoculars in his hand.

"Well, there isn't much. These buildings is like a wall to *everything else out there*, so why'd you expect me to leave?" O'Brien whistled, studying his arms to see if "Life" was the right description for him.

"Oh yeah, I've seen them. You're lucky you don't have raiders here, though. You'd get destroyed." The stranger haphazardly threw the binoculars and looked into the eyes of his old companion.

"Funny thing about being dead, excellent at playing dead. Bad thing about playing dead, some people aren't picky with their meat." O'Brien held up his hand to give Luke the finger, but upon closer inspection, that was the only remaining finger.

"So how've you survived this long anyhow? I had to do a dance with the devil just to keep myself fed, but how the fuck have you… stayed in mostly one piece?" He looked at O'brien's once bulky oil-stained frame and what it now receded to.

"The one part of me that didn't fade. My ingenuity."

"Well, it wasn't yours anyway, you stole it." From a fallen comrade, as all our gifts are earned.

"And I bet that's why I kept it! Same as you keeping your ability to eat rocks and shit."

"Oh, about that. I'm not dead."

"That would explain the body temperature and the blood and the every living part of you, pardon my eyes."

"Well, speaking of, would you happen to have seen an elderly man, getting older by the minute, going the same direction I was."

"The one that's dead tomorrow? Yes, he was at the square last my boys checked on him."

"That's all I needed to hear. I'll see you at the waterfront at eleven, old friend. Bring a gun, preferably high caliber." O'Brien merely smiled the devil's smile at him.

The old man tried to ask himself which one it would be. He saw the moving dust as an omen of his demise. All the fear he'd saved up for millennium was gushing out, the unknown was encroaching.

The news of the fight had already spread across the skyscrapers, and all the undead were chattering about the two men. Some rooted for the blithering old fool, but most saw what the traveler had in mind and figured he'd win by a landslide. The shapeless, dry wind guided Luke to the beginning, and on the same bench as it began, the old man curled and chittered his teeth.

"Friar." The old man jumped in fright.

"C-call, m-me b-by—" The lying old man couldn't even finish one of his once eloquently exaggerated sentences before he was cut off.

"I don't care who you were," spoke heavily the man who once spoke dumb and sweetly.

"M-m-milo. My name, was Milo." Smiled the Friar at the wind blowing past him.

"Well then, Milo. Why didn't you tell me I'd live with this?" The traveler misunderstood the deal.

"I knew it would be awful. I needed one stronger than I to live it." The cowardly teacher mumbled at the student, who now held his death in the palm of his hands.

Luke's fury peaked, higher and higher, shaking his arms almost out of their sockets. "Do you think this is stronger! Letting them die, seeing O'Brien that way, not dead and not living! Seeing that poor woman hung up like a fucking chandelier? Seeing the whole household you built get destroyed, the house that moved me away from my nothingness into a literal nothingness? Sharpening my knuckles on the walls of my cell, watching all my peers go crazy? Watching that poor woman get shot to death over a little box. Seeing the clouds grow and grow with his fire? Double suicide my ass, they would've been better dead! You fucked up the world because you could see the whole thing, huh? I would've taken those fucking eyes and ears you had if it would've made me choose different. You wanted to see how it'd turn out, like some sick game. You're just a curious little boy, aren't you, Friar? Found Daddy's matches, and now you think just because they're all gone you can cry. No, you don't get to cry. You don't get to cry until I find my pink medallion! Where would she have gone? Did you hide her? Hide her in one of those awful meals you taught me to cook, waiting for a time like this when I'm the only one well fed, you fucking god-complex-having vermin. Do you know what it feels like, caring for others besides yourself?" Every sentence held a punch at the end of it, finding their target simultaneously, so in sync that neither Luke nor the Friar saw the group of encroaching zombies.

"She's…with her sister. That is all I know, Luke. Trust me one last time." All Luke heard was the first four words, as they were interrupted by the Friar's lack of breath and the old man's heart beginning to stop, which was a faster transition than he would have ever imagined. So here was death, in all its shivering, bitter beauty.

Luke held O'brien's functioning hand and grabbed the gun out of the other. "We're a bit late to the party, ain't we? The whole cast was rooting for you, really, except for the ones that're a little older, but they ain't many. So now you're the only one living in the whole city, how's it feel?" A thousand emotions hit him all at once. His teacher was dead, his wife, and probably all the travelers he'd brought along for years, and now here he was, the commander of his city. The city he was born in, the one he'd grown up in, the one his first love was gained and lost, where his life had wasted away, and his sanity was abandoned, and most importantly, the home of the river. The river which carried him into a life of wonder and pain and everything he would never return to, but if he hadn't left, he wouldn't have returned. So absent of tweakers and peakers and whores and lowlifes and peasants and yuppies and hipsters, the city was his. Portland was the home of the dead and dying.

Human emotions had been washed away by years of death, the deadfellas, no matter whether they knew a man or not, they didn't quite empathize. That is why Luke gave him the jar of honey and said if he ever finds his pink medallion to deliver it to his honey. Go out with a pun, they always say. Going out with a bang too. That banging being caused by his steel-tipped boots balancing on the tracks as he walked to the railyard.

SAINT SALNO

This is just great. It's always great. I waste all the energy to
come out here, and she's gone. No trace. "Meet me down
by the river, we'll skip stones or something like that."
Whatever. She's lame anyway. Boring girl, nothing great about her.
She just wants to complain about him again. So here I am, kicking
my feet in the water like a kid, down by the river, where eventually
someone will come by and tell me that I can't be here, or the water is
too murky, or you look lonely or something.

See, I don't live around here. Me and Marcy, we been together
since, I don't know, I wanna say I met her when I was eight. She
would have been eleven then, and I don't remember her being that
old. Maybe it was before then. Point is, me and Marcy have been
friends for a while. She was this kid who wore flowers all over everything. She really liked them flowers. Hydrangeas, magnolias, roses,
all of them. She always felt kinda sad for roses, though. How they're
all thorny, and regularly they look dull and boring. When they're in
the bud form, I mean. Or maybe she really loved 'em, who knows.
It's been a few years since me and her talked about flowers.

So that's why I came down here. Was for Marcy. Take the two-
hour train ride here because she was having a problem with Jose.
Jose, she had to pick a Jose. Every Jose I've met has been a jerk or a
slacker or something. Okay, there was that one Jose who was pretty
cool. But it's been the same with everyone she's dated. I hate their
name. She has bad taste. I don't quite know what's wrong with Jose.

She just told me to meet her down here and we'd talk about some-thing. I'm assuming that's it.

So there I am, smoking a cigarette and kicking my feet, and there's this kinda old guy over to my right, fishing. It gets me think-ing, he has no idea why I'm here. I know he's here because he's fish-ing, he's got a line and a pole and a tackle box and all. Just because of his demeanor I can tell he probably isn't catching anything. Just look-ing at me, curled-up jeans, tank top, and a frown on my face, kicking my feet. I probably look like a wanderer. Haven't shaved since New Year's, so I can imagine it's pretty scruffy. I figure I'll talk to him. It's a sunny day, and I got nothing better to do until Marcy shows up.

"Catch anything, man?" I half shout, assuming he's farther than he is.

"Not anymore, you scared 'em all away. Heh, just kidding. I caught 'em well yesterday, but today they just ain't biting."

"Well, that's why it's called fishing-"

"Not catching. Old phrase, where'd you hear it?"

I thought for a minute. Where did I hear it? "Oh yeah, my friend used to say it a lot. We'd fish down by this crook when we were kids, and she'd always say that whenever I got down about catching nothing."

"Why didn't ya put a ring on it then? Sounds like a real keeper. Or are you a fruit or something?" Then he bellowed a chuckle, peered out of that one eye as if he could just tell whether or not I was a fruit and whether or not I was a dangerous fruit.

"Well, it's been a bit different now."

"Ah, I see. That's a real tale I'd like to hear over a brew. She pretty?"

"Well. Not really. She's strong and all. She has this weird beak-type nose. That ain't a bad thing at all, but most people don't really like that. You know, people would tease her about it. I guess it's attractive or something now, but I can only remember the teasing, so I don't really think of it as pretty. She's really thin too. That ain't a bad thing either, just kinda worrisome sometimes. I always worried she didn't eat enough, but she was in the track and all. Ran and ate like crazy. That's all she did in high school, was run and eat. Pretty tall too, blond. Well, she was blond. She dyed it red a while ago, and that looked fine. A weird change, but it looks nice. I don't know if she dyed it since."

"Oh yeah…hair dying. I never quite understood that. Sounds like you got a lot to say about her."

"Not really. Just known her a long time." The river gasped, as it could remember the times me and her shared here, and it was in on it all, as if it chose us back then to stay around this river, just the two of us, the best friends of the river.

"Well, you know, a long time is just a lot of words. Think about a sentence and how long that lasts. Imagine that over the stretch of time that is a year. It's a while, dude. Hell, if you could tell me everything about her, it'd probably take a year or two."

I sighed, taking a drag. Killing myself a little sooner. "Yeah, that's probably true."

"Now call me if I'm wrong, but you love this gal. Tell me what's wrong with her."

"Well, I wouldn't say that. I care about her. There's nothing wrong with her."

"Be honest with me, boy. You already got me curious. I've had three bites while we been talking, and I didn't reel in a single one because I'm curious. Now tell me what she done."

"Nothing, really. She's just popular."

"Is that what they call it now?"

"Call what?"

"Floozy, tart, whore, slut, all them things?"

"No. No. NO! She's none of that. She just doesn't know how to stay single, I guess."

"Well, I'd say that's on you then. That's the only issue?" His rod tipped downward again.

"Well, no. I'm not her type, you see. I've thought about it, I might have even talked to her about it. She just doesn't like guys like me."

"Like what? From the way you talk about it, she's had everything under the sun. What makes you so special you don't fit?"

"Nothing, I'm just…" His rod was pulled into the water, and he just sighed and started packing up his gear.

"Not confident. Go be confident. I'm packing in before the sun kills me. I met this babe down in Hawaii. She liked surfers. So you know what I did? I went to the shop on the other side of the big isle, and I bought the cheapest surfboard I could find, and I rode that like it was the only thing I knew to do. She still hated me. So you know what I did, I learned what she liked about surfers. It was their hair. I copied that, and she still hated me. Finally I asked what she hated about me and why I wasn't good enough, and she said, 'You're trying to be like my type, which is the worst kind of man.' So then I went and I surfed and I surfed and I just learned I really loved surfing, and she comes up and says hi and says she wants some of that, and I said, 'Nah. Takes too much time out of my surfing.' Now of course I still had the hots for her, I always did, but I didn't want to kill my pride to say I got good at surfing for her. So I didn't, because I didn't have to. I had the choice, after I forgot about it being a goal. That's how she was, I don't know much about American women. When you do see her, tell her to go look for the house of lights. Peace."

A Crippling Doubt

Dr. Strauss held a pen to her lips, listening to the poor man rant endlessly. She had met this patient just a few days ago and, due to a lack of other appointments, had seen him every day since. "And I don't know why she wants to kill me. Everywhere I walk, she's there with her pink umbrella and her fancy lacy shoes. I grow afraid every time I see those fancy shoes. You know I really wish I knew where I could buy them, and it's insult to injury that I can't ask her."

Strauss nodded and tried desperately not to daydream. She tried oh so desperately not to think about raccoons and their cute little eyes and how she very much wanted to tame one. It was always a dream of hers, to go to America and tame a raccoon. Of course they have them in England, too many for that matter, but she thought they would be nicer in America. She read Kerouac and his talk of raccoons and drugs and cheap food. It was a wonderful world in America, but she was far too old now to tame a raccoon. All this while Richard continued talking about how he wished he could talk to his murderer about her fashion. He went on talking about how if he could work that outfit, he would go by Rebecca and try not to murder anyone. But if he looked that good, he would have to bat the men off like flies. So she thought about raccoons in America, pretending she was listening. It was his money she was burning.

"You know, I rather enjoy ball gowns. I wore one to a party in college. A masquerade ball, so he couldn't see my manly neckline. He being the dashing young man who later threatened to stab me upon removing my garters. Oh, but it was so gorgeous. It had blue linen under it, and it was sparkly. If I wasn't such a pretty man, maybe she wouldn't want to kill me. Maybe, just maybe I'll ask her why she wants to kill me today. I see her everywhere, you see."

Richard raised his voice enough to make Strauss interject. She was thinking about finger painting with a raccoon, and in the middle of the paper stood Richard in a blue ball gown, bushy beard and all. "Now, how do you know she wants to kill you? From the sound of it, you two have never talked." Strauss cleared her throat promptly after as if to say she was listening.

Richard chuckled, twirling his somehow feminine beard. He made sure that even with a beard rivaling a mountain man, he made it fit his feminine physique. "Well, she's told me so. That's all she's ever said. I'll stand at the corner store, and I'll buy my sangria, and she'll get in line behind me and whisper, 'I want you dead.' It's terrifying, because I've never seen her face. She makes sure that whenever she is close to me, it's behind me. It's terrifying."

Dr. Strauss let out a sigh and wrote down on her notepad. For the first few days, she wrote down what Richard Meier had uttered infinitely. However, he stopped noticing the movements of her pen and just talked casually. She had learned the names of all his pets, his friends, family, and entire elementary school roster. She could state what he ate for dinner on Tuesdays, Thursdays, and Saturday, because those were the only days he ate out. She could tell you that his favorite moon is a waning gibbous, because he caught frogs best on those days during his childhood. She knew more about Richard Meier than she did her husband, which only existed in her mind, but still existed, mind you. "Richard, does this woman exist? Is it possible she is a figment of your imagination, which gets excited in public spaces?"

"Oh no, Doctor, she's very real. I've seen men hand her cards and other pleasantries. It's irritating how she gets more attention than me. Now, once one of her men did give me an up and down, you know. I saw his eyes and that God-given smirk after. Maybe I'll ask her for his details. You know, Dr. Strauss, that is a wonderful idea, I think I will go talk to her. I'll do that this instant, thank you." Richard ran off, smiling blissfully, and his heel angrily clicked upon the thirty more steps to the ground floor.

Before Julian Strauss could ask for a check, Richard had hobbled out the door. She suggested he stop wearing heels because of the size of his feet, which were 14 in men's department, 12 in women's. She swore it would be the end of him, and it would be. Julian wiped the sweat off her forehead and parted her silver locks. She had the unfortunate trait of early graying. It started when she was thirty-four and made her decision to go to college very problematic for her love life. Now, at forty-five, she looked as if she could be sixty minus the severe wrinkling. It was horribly irritating, and she cursed any higher being that could have caused this.

The next morning, the mailbox was again empty. The only piece of mail left was a sticky note that said to call Richard. Julian wondered why for the past week she's had no mail, and today she has a small note.

The phone rang and rang and eventually turned to voice mail with a click. She put on her coat and bicycled to the office in which she practiced. To her surprise, the parking garage of the building was sealed off completely by a line of police cars. All the bike racks were full.

"Excuse me, Officer, but what seems to be the commotion?" She interrupted a short dopey officer standing in front of the garage from his loitering.

The shrimpy, cheesy mustached cop replied to her meekly. "Well, you see, miss, it appears as though there may have been a little incident that happens to involve the, you know, life and death sort of thing. You know, the ones that breathe and the ones that pull triggers and the ones that don't breathe anymore because they were near somebody that was coincidentally pulling a trigger at the same time. Catch th' gist?"

"No, Officer, I can't say I do…"

"A moider."

Strauss gasped, because the most recent murder was several years ago in this area, the *competent police* here made sure no murders could occur. Apparently they missed them. "I work here, and I'm curious if this victim might be related to me somehow. You see, I had a patient, and he was worried someone was going to harm him, oh my flaming mother mary! How I should have taken it seriously!" She burst into mock tears, a skill she developed from years of being considered elderly.

"Well, our vic is a bit of a queer case, the men wearing dresses and pretty ribbon shoes and all."

"That would be Richard, if he has a large glossy feminine beard."

"He was shot six times."

"Oh woe is me! Wait, did you say ribbon shoes?"

"Lit'el pink uns, miss, too small for his feet it seems. He was shot when he was on the ground. He fell down the stairs."

"Oh, well then he couldn't have been wearing the pink shoes, because he was wearing heels yesterday. Red ones. That and he wears a 14 in men's, 12 in women's. If you can pull those shoes off him, I might be able to get you the identity of the killer. First swab them for skin flakes or whatever, then bring in a—"

"Listen, ma'am, you're hysterical, and we can't have any hysterics 'cause they'll attract lunatics, and lunatics attract sol-otics, and those are the ruddy worst, so don't be having any hysterics."

"What's a sol-otic?" Strauss asked jokingly, trying to gauge how much longer this fellow should be at the academy.

"Well, it's much like a lunatic, but you say it must be high noon rather than a full moon. That and sol-otics are associated with high noon, which occurs every day, and the full moon only comes, what, every two or some weeks."

A pickup truck crashed in the distance. "So you mean to tell me that sol-otics appear more often than lunatics?"

"Well, no. They're associated more often."

"Well, it isn't high noon. It's nine thirty."

"No matter how much you say it isn't high noon, it is certainly high noon."

"And why is that?"

"Because it's high noon."

"You're no help, I want to go into my building, and I want you to scrape my patient off the concrete and slap him a few times for getting killed. Then bring him in for a session, I'm lonely."

"But, ma'am, he's dead."

"*Then bring him in for a SESSION, I'm lonely.*" She clung to every syllable like a little girl clings to the dolls her mother tells her she's too old for, because she's in her thirties and hasn't even filled out an application for McDonald's yet.

Perhaps it was Strauss's hidden desire to talk to anyone but this speech-impeded cop, or the cop's brain chip shooting electrons toward a larger of its species, but a fat cop came shuffling toward them. To call this cop fat was almost a joke, because the cop was comically fat, bags of the stuff hanging from every corner of its body. It took every step as the unloading of a crane, the pools of fat dripping around the foot of its owner, only to be ripped from its new home a split second later. After a mere thirty-eight seconds, the cop was pointing its gaping head at the smaller of the two and uttering, "Wots the metter he-ere?"

"This woman appears to be working in this here building, Chief. She says that the dead fella might be one of her patients, but she hasn't given me a straight answer."

The chief's mouth opened wide, in a yawn or roar, showing his sporadically placed teeth to the two before him and then closed it again. With a slow subtle motion, he scratched a third of his ridiculous stomach and then hobbled back to his earlier position.

Luke was on the top floor of the parking garage, smoking a cigarette and smiling at the amount of cops there were. "So I suppose she finally cracked. I expected it, as usual." Then bit into a ground phonebook and mustard sandwich. The concrete rubble that Richard kicked up as he fell made a wonderful condiment to it.

"So if you'd like to make a witness testimony, there's quite a bit of explanation for how to get the paperwork and such, then the writing and—"

An American man walked down and out of the parking garage, unnoticed by cops entirely. This caused Julian to scream madly, "Why the hell did you let him into the garage then?"

"Who, miss?"

"That man right there!" she screeched, pointing to Luke, who was still nonchalantly pacing, only stopping to look in the direction of the screech. He stuck his tongue out and continued walking.

"Oh, well, you see, miss, he isn't in the garage."

"He just walked out of it!"

"We would've seen it if he had. You're beginning with the hysterics again. No, you can—"

Julian didn't allow the cop to continue talking to her. It's obvious that the bobbies were no help in this current circumstance, and having her only patient been murdered, who paid her handsomely, she needed to either find a new patient or find who murdered him. Either way, her first lead was the goofy-looking American who just exited her building of work.

Luke had made some casual distance, but he was by no means escaping her. He was actually just out to get groceries, make a sandwich, then go back to the scene of the crime. Maybe smell the blood stains and try to follow her, that gorgeous creature whom he saw murder that poor man. She smelled very nice, so it wouldn't be hard to find that scent. Like bark chips burning, slow roasting a bushel of roses, seasoned with liquefied toad. A very queer scent, but none the least bad.

Julian could only notice that the man had stopped in his tracks, and that gave her time to catch up to him. He didn't take notice until she pulled the old "I don't know you, but I don't like you because you're mysterious" routine. She actually said, "Look here, suspicious fellow, I don't know what business you had in my place of work, but I don't want to see you there anytime soon!"

"Not unless she shows up again, I don't plan on it. I can't recall why I was there in the first place actually. Did you happen to see where she fled?" Luke looked at her with no real interest. She wasn't old, but she wasn't young, and she seemed very boring.

"You saw her? There? So you can confirm *she* did kill him?"

"Oh yes, absolutely, it was a gorgeous crime. First she pushed him down the stairs then shot him six times from the top of the stairs. That's why one of the bullets is in his foot and not anywhere close. She wasn't aiming well. If he were luckier and landed face-first, then he would've survived. Horrible luck these people have." He was admiring a cricket perched on a stop sign.

"Then why didn't you call the police? Why didn't you tell the police, you walked right by them!"

"Well, see, that's a heavily loaded question. Me and police can't really formally interact, a bit of a deal I made a long time back. You wouldn't know anything about it because you're not crazy."

"You're…crazy? I'm a psychiatrist, and my only patient was just shot to death by a woman you seem to be pursuing." She smirked.

"Not interested in being cured." He smirked harder.

"I'm also very lonely." She adjusted her smile with a hint of coyness.

"I'm not interested in women of your profession." Luke adjusted his smile with confusion.

"Not that kind of lonely." Julian readjusted the smile upside down.

"Yeah, sure, now where'd she go?"

Julian looked at him quizzically and menacingly, as if to say she had no clue and he could go fuck himself. He looked back disappointed and triumphantly as if to say, that's a damn shame and you wish I would. Amidst this antagonism, there was a small mime in the far corner of the scene, pointing at the two of them its little finger gun. When the thumb trigger pulled back, the mime fell on his ass, and the children watching him laughed and threw pence into his hat.

Because Julian didn't have a job, she kept tailing Luke and was rather curious what a suspicious fellow like him was doing in England in the first place and how he came to be there at that time. Luke was curious why this bag was tailing him but always wanted an old woman to be fond of him. Maybe she'd start buying him presents eventually. Not to say he was anywhere near young, thirty-four wasn't really young nowadays. All his friends were either dead or married or married to death. The one that's married to death wasn't very close to him anymore, since death lives so far away, and she decided to move in with him. His age was showing, and it was awful.

A man like Luke didn't want pickles on his sandwiches. He didn't want normal things on his sandwiches. He liked jelly, kippers, and rat poison the most, very foamy. Julian, seeing him purchase this odd amount of items, was very intrigued, and so she uttered, "Are you suicidal, mister..." Ending the sentence as such, she hoped he'd fill in the blank.

"Just 'sir' actually. No, technically I'm not. Just my preference. I can eat quite a lot of things that should definitely kill humans. Rat poison, delicious. Most people of this sort will tell you blue-ringed octopus are the way to go, but they have hardly any flavor. Wait. Do you smell that?" Luke pressed his hand against the railing of the aisle, pointing his nose doggedly into the air.

"Your level of bullshit?" Strauss watched him scientifically.

"No, no. It's...her. The weapon isn't on her, but she's near."

The aisles of the store whispered to him with their scent. The scents of a thousand hands that may have brushed against the corner of a cereal box or the feet which pounded the floor eternally. Julian smelled odd to him too, indescribable at the current time, but smelled an awful lot like someone far older than her. But that scent of the woman he was pursuing, it was nearing him.

Three aisles down, the woman in question heard the hurried shuffle of feet. There were two pairs of feet, one moving fast and the other moving irregularly hobbled. She pretended they weren't aimed at her until they were about two aisles away, then she realized it had to be for her and dropped everything to run.

Conveniently, Luke could smell her begin to run almost a second after, because the scent was getting weaker, and their proximity caused him to hear her. Conveniently, Julian was paying more attention to her eyes and ran the minute she saw the woman dart out the nearest aisle. In that heavy pink fancy gown, with the pink hat and black, almost jet-black hair, Julian was certain that was the woman Richard had described. The store clerks dodged her, as the pair pursued her.

They were fast enough to keep up until outside of the store, but the streets held much danger. Mainly because cars existed, and this woman with the miniature pink top hat was very fast for her outfit.

The noon light was heavy, tiring, and far too much for Julian. After four blocks of running, she hunched over in exhaustion in front of a balloon stand.

Once Luke shook off Dr. Strauss, the journey was far more intense. It's almost as if the woman was playing a game with him, because as soon as the doctor fell back, she increased her speed and mechanics. It elevated to her climbing atop a parked car, jumping from there onto a fire escape, and climbing up the building from there. Luke couldn't copy her footsteps, but it wasn't too hard to get up the fire escape without climbing onto a car.

The old theory that a ball gown can make you hover if you're far enough off the ground or you jump high enough is incorrect. The same idea with an umbrella has caused so many would-be criminals a fall to their death. This woman did not make such a mistake. Once she was atop the roof, she leaped from it, onto the adjacent fire escape, barely catching herself as the dress seemed to be detrimental to her aerodynamics. Luke caught up to her on that end of the building but didn't want to jump, so instead he yelled, "You're beautiful and very good at murder!"

"I can say the same to you, oh stabber of hearts!" she threw out unromantically, still not at eye level with him.

"England really sucks!" He lowered his volume, watching her climb up the next level of the escape.

"Yeah, I know, but the States aren't any better, Luke." She made eye contact with him, and her eyes matched her suit, making everything he knew about eyes fly away, and upon finding a new folder for information empty, he decided he would learn.

"Oh, I'm glad you know me, but I don't know you."

"Some of the Friar's students choose to ignore their peers. I didn't!" She was finally at eye level, and her face was almost flawless. As Luke was used to with his sense of beauty, it was flawed. Her lips were very low on her face, giving it a serious, almost sad look all the time. Her eyes were pink, the kind of pink you would find on a rose quartz or a flamingo. Hot, medallion pink.

"Well I can see you chose speed. That's probably been rather helpful for things of this nature!" Now that he knew they shared the unearthly gifts, he felt more at home in her presence. It was almost as if they were having a chat over tea and biscuits.

"Immunity would have been more useful, that's what you chose, isn't it?" She daintily pulled up a pink glove.

"It really isn't all that nice, just a lot more choices for dinner." He had the audacity to wink at her.

"Why don't you come over here so we can chat privately? Reminisce and all." The same gloved hand beckoned him across the multiple story gap.

"I am certain you would either push me off the building or kiss me, not really sure you or I would want either of those right now."

"You're telling me the allure of the unknown and the allure of my lips don't appeal to you?"

"I'm telling you the allure of death isn't unknown to me, and I couldn't handle just a kiss."

"My, what a devil you are." She paced along the edge of the roof within speaking distance with him, tripping a few times jokingly to watch him squirm.

"Why'd you kill that…man. Woman. Person?"

She stroked her chin for a moment, as if she were pondering some ancient philosophy. When she arrived on the answer, a light-bulb nearly came into existence over her head, only to fall short and become a plate of grilled urchins instead. "Well, I'd been telling him—" And then the plate of grilled urchins cracked over her head, and she fell backward onto the grainy rooftop.

Luke didn't know what to do. There were several options here: Let her lie there only to escape when she wakes. Wait until she wakes, then surprise her. Bring her to Strauss to be questioned. It would be impossible to turn her over to the police; that's the bit that *is* impossible.

The Friar was a queer fellow. He'd been dead for years, and he didn't know until someone told him. His response was "Oh no, that won't work at all, sorry. How about a decade or two from now, say?" That's the kind of extraordinary person he was. His name was long forgotten, and so he went as the Friar. He was never a priest; he just wore a robe for a short while. He thought the name sounded romantic, so it stuck. How Luke became associated with him was a very strange incident indeed.

It was back in Portland, back where he was born, and where Carmen deserted him and where no one wanted him there and a bit after their short reunion. They didn't live happily very long. They were completely incompatible. He loved her too much, and she loved him too little, and so he was left a broken man. Such is the way of love, and such is the way of every beginning. It was in this fashion that he met the Friar.

He was gone after an argument with Michael, an explanation of his disposition, a mad-sounding explanation of the way he thinks and how he desires and other trivial self-referenced bullshit. Michael said he couldn't stand living with him, and so for a week Luke was wandering the streets. He found a nice little place to sleep every night where he could think, by Skidmore Fountain, where no one would find him, hidden in the crowd. It was in this area where he found Stacey, the man who taught him to roll a joint, which he hadn't learned ever for some reason. It was also here that he found a man in a white checkered suit who was walking a crocodile.

"Young man, I can't help but smell that you're in an unfortunate disposition. May I ask why?" The turkey-necked man beckoned, trying to silence the roaring of his prized pet. Luke looked back up at him, looked at the reptile, back to the smiling gent, and then rubbed his eyes.

"Oh, I'm sorry if I woke you. Sleep isn't something I do any longer, so I couldn't tell," the elder chimed again.

"I can tell, it's four a.m." If it wasn't obvious from the company around him or the wide open eyes, Luke hadn't been sleeping.

"Oh, you're probably curious why I'm out. Well, I was originally helping two lovers along their journey, but right now I'm here for you. You have nowhere to sleep but here, and so I believe that you are going to come with me."

Luke looked to his right, where a pockmarked junkie was sliding a needle into his bulging blue vein, crying not to be poked again. He looked to his right at the sleeping junkie, soon to wake and go berserk at any time. Then Luke gazed at the crocodile and the thin, wrinkly hand extended to him. He decided to pick the lesser of three evils, a disguise for the greatest of three evils, but what the hell.

The city lights wrapped around them as they strolled past the grungy piss-scented part of town. As if to dilute the madness, the Friar lit his pipe and inhaled deeply. "It's legal here, isn't it?" And then laughed heartily and offered the pipe to Luke.

"I don't understand why you're laughing." Luke hesitantly snagged the wooden pipe.

"All in due time. First, I must ask you who she was. Or he was. I can only feel the pain, not the gender." His constant smiling was ominous but not malignant. Luke scratched his greasy hair and then exhaled.

"Thanks for the hit, I don't have much."

"Well, I figured you'd need it after Carmen fucked you up so bad. Oh my, pardon the profanity." Luke looked the man in the eyes and noticed something odd. Whenever the man blinked, his eye color changed. Luke's breath was growing heavy and scared of this stranger. So he took another hit and relaxed his walking.

"I didn't say her name, man." He choked out, "What's this strain? Strong stuff."

"Orangutan guru-juice, a crossbreed. Stronger than anything in the states. It's 50-something percent THC. Oh, and that's just one of many tricks I can teach you. Breath reading. It's a weird concept. People have many possibilities of what they can answer a question with, but if the question is exact enough, then you can hear all the answers at once. There was another answer you didn't say, and I'm not offended by it, typically men dressed like me are looking for prostitutes out here."

Luke laughed harder than he ever had and let out the most confused "Dude" he could. This was a crazy night and crazy bud, and so he must be tripping hard. It took him a minute to process that the old man couldn't be a hallucination if he was supplying this funky junk, so his face returned to astonishment. The Friar's crocodile smiled. Luke thought for a moment he was laced.

"So why me? Why'd you seek me out if you had two lovebirds you could'a chatted with."

"Oh, because they are having a terrible time right now. She has severe posttraumatic stress disorder, and pretty soon he'll figure that out. Mind you, I was not at all directly involved in their little meeting. Just for a minute on the radio and him bringing up seeing me barely. Fate's a bitch like that. If I got directly involved, everything would have gone EXCRUCIATINGLY awful. Probably result in double suicide."

"Oh." The Friar snickered at him with large red eyes.

"That and your emotions are stronger than theirs. I'm very curious why, *very* curious why."

Before Luke could respond, they were at the waterfront. The place was abandoned, except for a few little souls bouncing around, from those who'd jumped off there. They weren't really attached to it, so much as no reason to leave. Tends to be the case with suicide. No hope for the future, even in the afterlife. "This, boy, is where I came from. The water."

"You're a mermaid?"

"No. I got here on a boat, and I'm leaving for Wales tonight. You can come with me and learn breath reading and emotion gauging and all that shit that you think is cool. There is something I think you'd find very interesting."

"And what is that?"

"You just answered yourself. Invisibility."

"What? How does that work?"

"Why don't you ask the two young men over there, watching the bridge go up a few days ago? They know fairly well."

"Who?" The Friar looked up at Luke, as he was a good foot shorter than him. His smile was wide, and his eyes glowed an electric green.

"Don't worry about it, I didn't say that to you."

"Sounds good, bro. I don't really understand what all that means, but I have nothing tying me here. To Wales!" Luke should've thought about his school friends, his few remaining family members, the girls who'd wanted to kiss him that hadn't, the boys that wished the same, and all the youthful, mirthful choices he could have picked. He didn't. He was high.

"One question before we go. Do you like talking to the police?"

"No, I hate 'em."

"Good, because you won't be able to anymore, not so much a rule as a physical impossibility."

In Wales, Luke found himself in a very large lighthouse in Manchester. The boat ride was fairly watery, a bit runny, and slightly moist. Luke spent most of it attached to the side of the boat, or hot-boxing the cabin. Four short days later, Wales greeted them foggily, in the month of January 2018.

There was no training at the House of Lights, so much as there was work and study. Luke had little interest in the faculties of his peers, who stayed in various parts of the lighthouse. This was the beginning of his impotence of magical studies. He preferred washing the walls and cleaning the house and decorating more than meditation, more than occult practice. To say the Friar was a teacher would be very wrong. The Friar simply refused to be a realist, and so he had a very old crocodile and didn't decide to die yet. This caused him to ignore so much the laws of reality and helped others learn to as well.

In the following march, a woman named Delphine was inducted to their halfway home. This Delphine would be the woman presently lying on the couch of Dr. Julian Strauss, but then she was oh so very different. The Friar offered various gifts. Not so much gifts as unrealities. He offered to Luke the ability to breathe fire, which didn't appeal to him. He offered Luke the ability to be invisible, which was the initial reason Luke decided to come with the Friar. Once the gift was explained, that it isn't so much invisibility as it is curving attention away from yourself, he was uninterested. The irony of this is the Friar knew that was not the gift Luke would choose. He knew that was what would entice him. After tasting this wonderful English herb, what Luke truly desired was an end for the munchies, an end for poison and an end for pain of the mind and body. This gift was titled immunity.

Unlike most deliverers of supernatural gifts that are supposed to have a code and an order and some business to do with security, the Friar didn't really care. All his pupils were adults to be left to themselves. He merely gave them the gift. Pupils were constantly coming and going, and it was in this fashion that Delphine was brought in.

Delphine had no real interest in this garbage. She wanted to do things in a hurry and do a lot of them. So speed was the way to go for her. Each gift came with a great cost, mind you, and her cost was envy, a constant growing envy for those similar to her that wouldn't perish until she did. Her envy was beauty, though she had quite a bit of it. It was the thing that caused the death of Richard, and it would be the death of her, the Friar assured her. After staying not long, she left the House of Lights and went off on a journey. Really it was just stealing countless things for a decade, gambling and making heaps of money under false names. Such is the way of quick-thinking people. This weakness was easy to deal with in comparison to the weakness of the immune.

It wasn't until Luke was staring down at his scrumptious guest of his guest hood when he remembered her name. She had changed quite a bit since their last meeting, which was hardly a meeting so much as a brief hallway confrontation. Her eyes had changed. Strauss was in her kitchen making tea for three, because it was oh so pleasant to finally have a reason to break out the fine china. Luke was admiring her, so pale and fair and covered in grilled urchin sauce, which gave a nice touch to her original oddity of an aroma. Strauss only noticed his mutterings, his whispers into her unconscious ear, inaudible to any but her.

"What are you doing to that poor murderer, Lucas?"

"It's Luke, and I'm just telling her about me, so she'll know when she wakes up." He continued stroking her raven hair.

Before the doctor could retort, the girl rose up quickly, headbutting Luke back into his chair. She looked around like a deer in headlights then noticed the tea instantly placed before her and jumped away from it in absolute fear. She then looked at Luke and said, "I didn't want to know all those things, you're a creep."

"It's what I do, had to snap you out of it somehow." His smirk could burn down bridges.

"If you paid attention to the Friar's explanation of waking life and sleeping life, you would have been able to tell I wasn't sleeping." She spoke moving her hands back and forth with every syllable, like seeing them in motion would exert the point better.

"Why would I whisper such sweet nothings to a sleeping woman?"

Strauss had the most awkward smile placed on her face, watching these youthly folks have their reminiscence. It curled upward at a dire angle, in a mix of confusion, disgust, uncomfortableness, and envy, all this caused by curiosity. She didn't understand how these people were associated and what it had to do with the murder and why the murder was not the utmost concern. She made it the utmost concern.

"Just another cold body, ain't nothing special. Now this rose here, she's a real rarity," Julian sort of sang while bending to place the sugar on the coffee table. "How do you know her?"

"He's a creep who studied at my college, nothing more and nothing less," Delphine unceremoniously introduced him. "Hey, lady, that's a pretty scarf. I've decided I want it."

"But it's my only scarf." The look on Delphine's small face did not change, even as her hand jutted out to rip the scarf from Julian's neck, giving the woman whiplash. It was a feathery wool scarf, actually rather ugly. Luke took a moment to pull a large wad of various kinds of currency from his pocket, counted out enough to feed a family of four for a decade, and placed it next to the sugar dish.

"Don't worry about Richard, dear Julian. Thank you for the medallion," Luke flirted and ushered Delphine off the couch.

The sun began to dip toward the horizon as Delphine got up to go. Luke followed her from a distance, and Strauss remained in her office mixing whiskey into her expresso. Delphine ignored the fact that her high heels were gone, as well as her purse and everything important she had in it. All these objects were sitting in Strauss's tiny office safe, which Luke had found the combination to. It caused Delphine to seek out these objects. Strauss had completely forgotten about her, now misdemeanor majoring mime-mounted bicycle.

There was a light rapping at the door, just before Strauss could finish her drink. Outside the door she heard three pairs of feet stomp, and only two of them were human. "I could use a drink if you're up to company, Julian," an old singsong voice called outside of her office door. For some reason, be it fate or be it curiosity, she opened the door.

GRAVE DANCING THE WALTZ

Ticktock. Tocktick. The seven-hundred-dollar ornate clock chimes back and forth at the drop of the hour. It is now two o'clock in the afternoon, and there has been a death in the family. It happened several days ago, and here is the reading of the will.

"It has been brought to my attention that one of your ilk has passed most unwelcomely. I am visiting you in deepest mourning and hope that the reciting of this document can soothe your dusty spirits." The judge of last finances sputters on. I've never right liked these folks, getting paid to hand out the last pinches of someone's property. How they can read a paper and stare calmly at the lucky survivors who grin widely at the bags that are dropped on them.

"This will was written June twenty-sixth, eleven days ago today. This was signed by the late Jeremy Satchens, for whom we are all gathered."

Old Uncle Jeremy. He would have hated this little skit. He probably would've laughed at the drooping ears of this little man reading his last words. Hell, he might be laughing away next to me with a bottle of heavenly scotch in his hands.

"Dearly beloved, I am terribly sorry to say that I croaked. I really thought that I'd see it through to the end, maybe make a martini in the last ten minutes or something. *I'm reading the will, to remind you,* but I didn't, and so here you fuckers are wanting my money."

Ah. Jeremy. My favorite uncle. I remember when I first met him. It was the day of my father's funeral. It was raining, as to be expected in Washington, and everyone was sitting in the metal folding chairs in front of the hole where Roy Satchens was to be laid to rest. Everyone was all in order when the final rites were read. There was one empty chair at the front row, with a name tag on it. That name tag read, "An Ordinary Can of Soup."

"So here's the gig. I don't really have much. I have my dogs, which my woman will be keeping until they come meet me down here. Rachel is taking the boat because I've been trying to get her out on the water for seventeen goddamn years. Tell her if she sells it, I'm going to haunt her until her final breath."

My father was being lowered, about halfway down, and a jolt of lightning hit maybe three hundred feet away from the cemetery. Everybody looked around, startled and confused, but it didn't seem to bother anybody. At least anybody that was there. There was a loud "Holy shit, I'm glad I wasn't touching the fence! I'd be a little too buzzed to come in today!" from behind, which caused us all to turn. A tall man, maybe six feet, seven inches, or more, in a grimy motorcyclist's jacket and torn slacks, a flask in each pocket, smiling like the devil, walked into the ceremony. "It's okay, I'm low sodium." He jabbed at the priest as he removed the name tag, waiting for him.

"To Robert, Tell him he owes me thirty-five bucks, and I have thugs on the wire ready to come get it." From the direction of my cousin Robert, I heard a nervous cough and the sliding out of the chair. "I'm not getting into my estate because it's all going to Roy's kid. He's a silly little tyke that don't know shit about living on his own, so I'm sure it'll help him out. Make sure he knows that his promise is still valid and to bring his lovely whatever-the-fuck out there too."

"So hey. I want to say a few words for Roy. Daddy, lemme up there." He clutched the podium, smiling dryly at all the frowning branches of our burning family tree. It was obvious the priest and others at the funeral didn't much like this character, and I wasn't surprised I'd never met him. "So you're all here for my deadbeat brother, huh? Don't mind the pun. Well, for all of you that got dragged here and didn't know him, he was a stuck-up fuck. Ever since we was kids, he's been tattling on me, taught me not to drop the soap before tossing me in the slammer. That's what you get when your brother's a dirty cop. Now it's obvious I'm not gonna stand up here to tell you he was a good man. I seen too many poor kids lose their shit at his hands. But I won't tell you he was a bad man either. He did what he had to do to survive. Clearly, it wasn't enough."

The elderly man shuffled his papers, and the crowd stared at me. I hadn't come into any money like this ever. Sure, I tried my hand at gambling, and I made a bit of luck, but nothing like this. His whole estate, a nice house, sixty-five thousand dollars, and a hen-house. It was mine, except for the dogs. Strange thing about Jeremy was, he can't handle dogs. He hated them, but he had two anyway. He named them Terrible and Worse, and it figures he'd leave them to his wife, to whom he had been separated thirteen years.

Jeremy stepped off the podium, still grinning madly at the glares from the audience. Sure, there was more to the speech, but the majority of it was summarized there. He laid it all out on the table. He told us all about the constant "missing" evidence of cronies that would have never got convicted anyway. The money that left the occasional thieves' pocket in exchange for freedom. The way some of the prettier gals got out of speeding tickets. It was so awful that my mother was crying, and my aunt Georgette was praying aggressively. I was in shock, being young at the time, but not necessarily astonished. My father had always seemed like a wealth of wisdom and treachery to me. Uncle Jeremy knew all these things because he got the short end of the stick.

"Hey, kiddo. I only know you as my nephew, I don't know your name. Come over here a minute." Jeremy gestured to me. The view was marvelous, a lanky drunk and a confused boy half his size walking out of cemetery gates. Could have been a poem. The funny thing I always remember about Uncle Jeremy was the way he would talk to people. He would bend his legs, and with me he had to crouch, to make eye level with them. He found eye contact very important. He had dead, wild eyes. The weak pupils, vision distorted from years of second sight, were almost gray. He had an aging, tangly beard that stretched up around his mouth and hung over his lip like a dying cat. "So, uh, Jesus, I hate forgetting names. Alejandro? Josue? Juan? Rodrigo? Saldevar! That's it, Sal my old boy."

"My name is Isaac."

"Okay, we all make mistakes. I just figured you weren't really Roy's. I know your old bag loves to hang out down on those sandy beaches of me-hico. Different story, different time. How do you feel about your old man passing?"

"He drank and beat me."

"I should have expected so much. Wait. That was a joke, wasn't it, you little devil."

"I was second guessing that myself, looking at you."

"You're a witty little shit, I'll give you that."

"So what's up, strange relative?"

"Jeremy." He had a pathetic handshake. Weak, clammy, and wiggly. He promptly took a swig afterward, sitting down on the curb. I did the same thing. He was such a black sheep from my family. We cared a lot about face. This little bit of fun he had ended up getting him exiled by everybody but me. Even his own kids didn't much like him after all that. Half of us thought he lied; the other half thought that Roy's corruption wasn't any of his business. The latter half was just as corrupt. Happy family.

"You know, Isaac, I really don't see any reason to cry. I mean, look around. We have this water falling from the sky, this cold earth under our feet, and oxygen in our lungs just waiting to become laughter. So why the hell would we waste it on crying? I threw in a couple one-liners in there, hoping somebody would laugh but…the sadness is just too strong. He doesn't even deserve this much sadness, he was *such* a dick."

"Who decides who's worth crying for?" I chimed in. His head turned in his hands toward me and curled another smile. I can't remember if I cried that day.

"Good point, lad. Any other kook would say the Lord or something. But the ones who decide who to cry for are the ones who cry. I decided he ain't worth crying for, so I ain't crying."

"What do you hope will happen when you die?"

He thought for a moment, as another thunder rolled along in the distance. "I won't."

"But everyone dies."

"Who said that?"

"My dad, my mom, doctors, teachers—"

"And they will all die. Because they know they're gonna die."

"But don't you know you'll die?"

"Why would I? I'm not dead, and the only thing that we ever really…feel, singularly, is what's happening right now. Right now, I'm alive, it's raining, it's thundering, and there's a bunch of dipshits behind us. That's it. I will never die, as long as I continue living in the present."

Jeremy's house was mainly empty. There were a few loose objects, an empty briefcase, a lot of pots full of dead plants, and a mattress. The man had a four-bedroom house, and he slept in the living room. A worn, sheetless mattress, full of holes and loose springs, lay next to a shattered laptop and a portable printer. I suspected this was where he had lain when he wrote his will. The kitchen was full of empty bottles and strange refrigerator magnets. One of them read, "Allah's well that ends well." And captioned a picture of a suicide bomber jumping into a water well.

I kept exploring the house. There was nothing upstairs at all. He labeled the rooms, though. One of them read Kelly, another read Rachel, and then Terrible and Worse. They were barren, dusty, unopened for many years.

"So I took the anchor, and I tied it to the guy's corn. He says to me, 'Why did you put an anchor on my corn?' And I said, 'The Tuesday market is open every Thursday at six o'clock' and walked away." Jeremy roared into laughter at his own nonsense. I just kept on eating my ice cream.

"But that doesn't make any sense!"

He paused his hysterity for a moment to say "But nothing else makes sense, so you might as well laugh at it!" then kept chortling like a madman.

"Oh okay then. I think I got one. So I'm listening to two secretaries at work. The first one says, 'That seed was so delicious, I think I'll call him again tonight,' and the other says, 'Ooh, gimme his number,' so the next day I drop my number on her desk. That night I get a call, and I greet her with 'I have too many acorns, I hear you like a good nut.'"

"A fine specimen, but a good joke shouldn't have a punchline," Jeremy warned, wagging his stubby finger.

"Why is that?"

"Because then you can expect it. You figure, oh, they're talking about semen, so you're probably gonna throw in a play on words about tree seeds or something to that effect. A better end would be 'I heard you like a good nut, I have a 1970s Toyota for sale with minor headlight damage and a three-year-old raccoon pelt stapled to the roof of it,' so she'd be more confused and you'd laugh. *The person telling the joke should laugh the most.* What else is there if you don't laugh at your own comedy?"

I hadn't found any of his material. I don't think he ever wrote it down. He never did much with his jokes, besides tell them in inappropriate situations. The backyard was devoid of grass. He made sure there was no grass. In the week from his death, the grass had started to crop up. A damn shame.

The more nights I slept there, the more I began to be unsettled. Somewhere in the house, there was a loud banging. He didn't have an attic, and I remember I hadn't checked the cellar, which was only accessible by the outside. I cast aside all my fear of spooksome atrocities and hobbled in the dead of night to the cellar door.

On the door to the cellar, something was smashing its head against it. Something was trying to get out. It was then that I noticed the sign hanging loosely on the handle. It read, "Leave the pig and the rope be, I want it to be funny." When I unlocked the chain on the cellar, out burst a large potbelly pig, snorting and squealing loudly. Where the fuck did my uncle get a pig?

It was a common thing for me now, to go get ice cream and drinks with my uncle. I was twenty-two, and he was an aging man. The appeal of it never changed. I was still a child, and he was still an odd man. But this day was something different. He didn't have many jokes. No conversation, no rude comments on the population. Just the one-word answers in response to my inquiries. I ran out quickly. He normally guided these meetings. It was late, and we'd moved from the ice cream parlor to the tipsy torture tavern next door. He was three rums in and said, "The present ain't gonna last, is it, Ike?"

"Well, what all do you mean, Jeremy?" Rum was full of snakes and oil.

"I mean, look around. You're different than when I met you, this bar is different than when I first came in. You look different on a microscopic level than you did ten minutes ago. It's just…all goin'. Always moving. We never have the present. Our concept of the present is just the very, very recent past, because as soon as we, as we get it, it's gone. It all just poofs away. In a snap. Just like that. It's a drag, man."

Something was wrong. I knew something was wrong because I can watch him. He kept getting jollier and jollier up until this day. That's what he did when shit got tough. He would make it a joke. It had to be a joke. But when they all stopped laughing, the joke wasn't funny anymore.

"Ike, please do me a favor. I finally figured it out."

"Figured what out?" He stared into the empty glass, and I felt it. He didn't have to say it, and he did anyway.

"Figured out I'm gonna die. I guess you can call this the abyss, or belly of the beast, or whatever a little smarty like yourself can call it. The time when the phoenix burns up."

"But the phoenix always comes back." I saw a slow tear roll down his face, never reaching the bottom before it dried up. Half of me was surprised that he'd realized this, and the other half of me really believed that he would never realize he'd die. He never talked about it ever, in the many years since that day. That doesn't mean he didn't think about it.

"But this phoenix doesn't want to rise up, Isaac. This ash wants to ride the wind. To finally see what all the fuss is about. Just do me this one favor. I want you to write me a damn funny obituary, and I want you to dance on my grave. I don't want no drunken partying, though I wouldn't mind it. I just want some proper ballroom dancing. They'd never let me into one, so I never quite learned. Maybe If I did, it would have worked out different."

It's funny how we think about things in years. The older you get, the harder it gets to separate the years. He probably dropped an anchor on me that first day, decided right then that we'd end up right here, years and years later, and he'd be glum and sad and dying, and I'd be the same kid I was then because you can't really grow up when a parent dies. You just stop growing. Your brain doesn't stop, your body doesn't stop, but any impact that parent would've had to shape you stops. Guess it cured me. Of what, I can't tell.

The basement smelled like pig shit and gunpowder. In the corner of the room were cheap fountain fireworks. In the center of the room was a noose, hanging from the drain pipes.

"Jeremy Satchens was a real joker. He'd look at a fellow in a car and make up the longest, most overspun life you could ever hear that probably wasn't true. One of his best friends died, and he laughed. He had some dogs for so many years, just to laugh at how much he hates dogs. He took me in, living with my waste-of-space mother wanting me to get into accounting, and said, no, that kid's an artist. That kid ain't crying because he knows his dad's a piece of shit, not just a corpse in a box we should all cry over. But this ain't about me. This is about Mr. Jeremy Satchens, the fellow who laughs in the face of lightning and has a staring contest with the devil. Looking at the turnout here, I can see some of you had poor humor. He went out the way he lived every day, as a joke. He lit off fireworks and stood on a pig so he'd be laughing in his last few minutes. The best jokers laugh the most at their own jokes. It was pretty funny, Jeremy." I read to an empty crowd.

"It'll be okay, son. He's at peace now," the priest said, putting his hand on my shoulder.

"Ain't I a little old for ya, Father?"

I've never laughed and cried before. I hired a hooker to dance the waltz with me, on this stormy night, on my uncle's grave. She doesn't know why I'm crying or why I'm laughing, but she knows that I'm paying her, and she's had worse. I'm a real chip off the old block. Sorry it couldn't be classy like he wanted.

His headstone read, "Jeremy Satchens, 1956–2016. Life's a big joke. Everybody else down here right now, they didn't know that. Somebody *please* draw a dick on my headstone."

ON THE OUTSIDE LOOKING IN

The man with the green teeth slams the door on my fingers again. The light bulb hanging above my bunk is flickering again, and one of my left knuckles is broken. I would be able to inspect it properly if the only light above me isn't flashing on and off every five seconds. At this hour, anybody I could talk to about it is either sedated or asleep.

The green-toothed man smokes a lot of opium. I'm guessing he's about thirty-two, because he looks fifty and smokes a lot of opium. Earlier he was banging the metal plates together against the bars of all the cells, and all the druggies around me were expecting to get their fix. That's what half of the people are here for, fighting for. A fix. Trade a life of starving outside in the rain for one sleeping on a metal platform with a blanket and the drug of their choice. It seems like an acceptable deal to me.

So I made a splint for my finger out of a broken pair of chopsticks the guards forgot to take out of my cell. I'm not so sure that a splint will even be of use for a broken knuckle but whatever. Hopefully it will help in some way. If not, I'll just have to block with my right and swing left. Not that it matters, nobody else here fights clean. I'm the only one here with any decency and respect for fighting. It's an art, you know, a kind of pact between both parties. You're both there for the same thing, to take hits and deal blows, hoping to make all the people watching yell, "Good show!" But none of the boys around me know that. When they're in the cage, they see their toxin lying directly under their opponent's skin. Somewhere upstairs, Frank Sinatra beckons me to the moon, on an age-old vinyl player.

I'm trying to get them to give me a pillow. They say it's a toss-up between me and the guy down on the north wing who knows how to make an excellent pasta salad. That's all he ever dabbled in, was cooking. Not enough money for ingredients, when you're on the streets, you have to make decisions. He's old, very old. He's lanky, hunched over, and bearded heavily. He looks like nothing, but see him in a fight, I swear. There's a reason he's here. If he couldn't throw down, then he would've been thrown out. I've wanted to meet him. I only hear the bits and pieces that are thrown from the other end and what my cellmate knows.

Crong is asleep. He got his heroin and so there's no use talking to him. I've tried to write tonight, but nothing important is coming up. I thought about fish for a little while, only goldfish. I never had any other kind of fish, I only ever had the goldfish. In this neat little bowl that my mom bought me, a time ago. She set the bowl on a bookcase that was a rectangle sitting on its skinny end. I would get home from school, and I would look to see if my goldfish had ever gotten bigger, but it never did until I left. I wonder how the fish is doing, days like these. When the day seems like it won't ever end, when I look up at this concrete ceiling, gently vibrating from the blasting speakers upstairs.

Around 5:00 a.m., a man started screaming for his ankles, how they were missing and how someone had stolen them, and he wouldn't stop shouting until he got to the bottom of it. What little sleep I had ended there. In approximately twelve hours, I would be in the cage, looking another man in the eye and waiting for the bell to be rung. Until then, I try to write.

Every day here is the same as the last. You fight every night. Sometimes you don't come back, but usually not. It's bad for business to have someone die. They don't frown on it, because people will bet higher when there's more blood, but they really only want carnage, not death.

I only call the green-toothed man Mr. Green, appropriately. He's just a warden; he has no power. He brings us to the cage, and he puts us back. He doesn't care if we won or if we lost, because in the long run, he got paid. I used to drink when I first got here, but fighting with a hangover is no fun, so I don't drink anymore. They don't give you enough water to mix with the grog anyway.

My cell is swung open, and the salty, sickening scent of Mr. Green's trench coat is stuck to my nostrils. He doesn't bother with a Taser or a spear or some other long-range weapon to make sure you don't escape. He has a gun, a very large one, that he keeps in the pocket of his coat so that it hangs out and you can see how large it is. Large enough to put a seventeen-inch hole in the strongest torso. He doesn't tie your hands up. Whenever he's had to use it, I always close my eyes. I hate the sight of blood.

You never hear the sound of a car crash when you're in the car crash. You never hear the sound of a bloodthirsty audience, ripe with ill will toward whoever they're betting against unless you're in the ring. You don't feel the dust and blood and bits of torn clothes and sweat under your feet unless you're in the ring.

You look at who you're fighting. A tall man, shirtless, cut the hell up all down his body. He's probably been shanked once or thrice by those who found a way to make weapons. They aren't disqualified, it's called ingenuity. He's bald and has a tattoo around his eyes to mimic raccoon spots. His hands are dirty, and he's curling them as if he's squeezing a ball rather than making a fist. That's how I can tell he's not going to try and hit me. He's going to try and throw me.

The gong was smashed, and the crowd roared louder than before. There is something peculiar worth noting about tonight. It's tonight I decided that I was going to die. Normally when he steps toward me, I move away or block or hit back or something, but I just didn't feel like it. Seeing his black-eyed face, scrunched with emotion and awaiting intoxicants on the other side of me, took all the fight out of me. You don't ever feel a car crash when you're in a car crash. That's where fights and car crashes differ. You can always feel someone grabbing you by your arm and throwing you across the cage into the sharp blood-covered rust. My arm was at an angle that I didn't want it to be, and the pain had stopped me from realizing that I was still being hit. His empty hand slammed my head into the cage and picked me up, still holding my battered face to show the crowd his trophy. He threw me against the cage again, scraping my forehead down the rusty bar. He left me with a heavy kick to the ribs then stood victorious before the crowd.

Mr. Green doesn't care whether you win or lose. We all go to the same place, reused for the same reason. My arm was bent backward, dislocated or broken or worse. One of my ribs was broken, and my face was bleeding from the gash in the middle of it. I wonder what I looked like then, staring at that pompous, enthusiastic fat audience. They are all the same as a crowd, just raw hunger for gore, coming from a fat, wealthy face. That's what they all look like to me, even though I know they aren't all that, because I know that many of them are people I would have liked to know, if I was on their side. These are the thoughts I have as I lay bleeding on my blanket, estimating the amount of blood loss per second to know when I'll die.

"He's dying, Jess. Tybol the claw took him here, got him in this sense of shape, Jess. He didn't even hit back, You've got to look at him," a voice from outside of my hazy vision says. It sounds like sunflowers, like tall wheat in the sunshine and a cold beer waiting for me.

"Oh, what a poor shape our doll is in, isn't he?" a darker voice speaks. A longer voice, a deeper but more real voice says. I can smell the sensuality in it, the morbid curiosity for my condition.

"Look at that, it's sticking out and all," Sunflowers whispers.

"Oh my, at such an angle. And look, his face is torn. A patch will do there just fine."

"Jess, he looks awake."

"Perfect, I love snapping them into shape when they're awake to thank me." As the dark voice speaks, soft hands wrap around my morphed forearm. On the word *snap*, my arm is twisted forward, the sound of bone scraping bone emits. In shock, You don't feel these things.

"Jess, what's his name? This one didn't fight at all." Sunflowers is resting her calloused fingers on my toes.

"Oh really? I'll ask Donaldo when I go down to the office. Hand me the thread, will you. I need to sew up his head before he bleeds out."

It took maybe an hour, maybe three, maybe less or more, but I was alone again. Lying in the same place, only more uncomfortable now that I had a splint. I was in excruciating pain, and whenever I winced, my forehead crinkled and caused more pain. I was in constant agony that night.

I dreamed of clouds and of happiness. I wasn't sure what happiness was, so I envisioned it as a woman. A beautiful woman, with long hair. But she wouldn't look at me, she didn't want to listen to me, and she wouldn't sing or speak or dance. She merely stood constantly ahead of me, with the clouds around us floating through the sky and the ground. I wanted to speak, but there was a towel in my mouth, the same towel they put in my mouth when it bleeds.

I don't know what time it was when I awoke, but the sunflower voice was in my room again. "Salno, why didn't you fight?"

My eyes were closed, and the clouds sunk, and here I was, staring at the woman who finally turned toward me, and I saw she had no face or ears or even fingers. She was merely a husk of a woman. She was nothing to me.

"You didn't answer me, and I can tell from the way your eyes move that you are awake."

"I don't want to be alive anymore."

"Salno, you know that that isn't allowed here."

This woman didn't have the mock-curiosity to her voice from earlier. She sounded like she pitied me, and I hate pity.

"Salno, are you lonely?" Her fingers dinged slowly on the bars with each syllable.

I thought about the word. What did lonely mean. It made me think of basketball. I lived near a basketball court, one that was broken and abandoned and hardly a flat surface, with a broken baseboard. I played ball there, but always alone. The other boys would pass by and look at my ball playing and then keep walking. That was loneliness.

"Yes."

"Salno, what is your drug of choice?"

"It should say on my file, miss." I faked politeness. Why?

"I read your file, it's very interesting. I wanted to hear the words from their speaker rather than a medium."

"It should say," I ground out, tired of her being there. Tired of my clean air being divided for two, as rare as it was in the cages.

She ran her fingers along my shaved head, almost raising feeling from it. As her index finger neared my eyebrow, she pressed down heavily on the stitching in my head. "Please?"

"Books." My servant mouth let escape.

"And where are they, Salno?" she queried. I felt like she was looking me in the eyes, but my eyes were still closed. Amidst the night whisperings, night ravings, and tweakers banging themselves against the bars, her voice poured like honey into my universe. One that had been in a cell so long it had lost the taste of sweetness.

"They've never told me. They gave me paper and said if you wish for books then to bloody write one." I remember my swindlement.

"Salno, why are you here?" Salno, why am I here?

She had lost her false sincerity and had become genuinely curious. The door to my cell closed slowly, and she sat down on the edge of my bunk. Where her hips pressed against my calves was warmer than anything I had felt that wasn't a fist or a leg or a stick or anything that had hit me in my memory.

"Salno, sweet Salno. How did you end up in a place like this?" She touched my chin, my cheeks, my neck. I despised it, this gentle touch. It hurt more than anything, and I wasn't sure why. My eyes hurt, and they twitched. My throat welled up, and air that should have been there was not. A noise rose from my throat, and then I realized I was crying.

Donaldo didn't come for me today. Perhaps they were shuffling off the boys. Trading them out for new ones. I was waiting for them to kill me, to know I was too broken to fight. The cages opened, and the cages closed, and I counted the times they opened and closed, but never once did mine open. When the meals were served, after the fights, I got mine late. I didn't eat it. I gave it to Crong, who had his eye gouged out today by a very sharp thumb. He thanked me heartily, hoping it gave him the energy to grow it back, the poor Neanderthal.

I lay there all day, and all night. I awaited that cold sound, the hope that the door would open and I could fly free. It was late when the door opened once more. "Salno, where is my book?"

"I haven't written one. I never will. Unless you're going to hang me, go away please," I uttered out, enough for her to hear me.

"Open your eyes for me, dear."

"No."

"What do you have to lose? Are you afraid I'm in your head? Are you afraid I'm prettier than my voice implies?" she teased me, shuffling my empty papers around.

I hesitantly opened them. Nothing was on the table that I hadn't already lost. This woman had never talked to me for the past several years, so why was she here again? She was thin, looked dangerously so, but still alive, draped under a black lab coat. Her eye was false, one of them. It didn't move when her other moved, but it was a different color, so I knew it wasn't lazy. Her head was also shaved, and she smiled at me. Her lips were full and had cuts all across them. She was so pale, and she looked so broken as well. Her voice did not match her, the sunflowers that once were now shriveled in sight of the sun. Her eyes didn't match her or each other.

"I am not what you expected? I never hid from you, and yet your face says it all. Well, how about it, champion. I keep you fed until you heal and let you live as long as you write me a book."

"No." I shot the servant pulling the strings, point-blank, and watched the poor fool bleed out just for following orders.

"That is fine. That wasn't a request, that is what will happen. You have a long time to do it, you're sold in for life, you know. I will return tomorrow. I have the night shift, so this is the only time I can see you. I can see you."

When she said that, she stood up and left in the same swift, deliberate way she had the night before. I hated her. She brought me memories, which are never a thing you want. It's like a rat, if you let one be, it will bring others, and they will repopulate and get larger and then take you over. It was like this, that a rose grew in dusty soil.

Sunflowers and daffodils and every bloom in the world danced before me, in colors of a hundred different crayons, all used up from years of dreaming. All the flowers which I had seen, floating so gently, and one stood proud among the others, a rose. A simple bloom, not the prettiest of roses, but it smelled so sweet, and its thorns were not so sharp. It rested downward, less bright than all the others. I plucked it and smelled it, and its thorns pricked me. I bled so much, so much to drown the other blooms, and yet none of it stopped me from breathing. I floated in the ocean of petals and sanguine, crying for all things I found holy.

The petals faded, the blood dried, and in place of it was the morning. The morning was cold and darker than it should have been. I stared at my notepad, set still on my bunk, untouched and staring back at me. It told me to write in it, to create an outside, one that had wind and trees and ears and breath and tongue and a valley of buffalo wandering its white padded walls. And so I tried to reach for it. My left knuckle was still broken, and my right was in a cast.

To explain the death of Erin, it began with the hours of shrieking. That was like a cock-crow here, and they resided in the walls until five, when the fights began. I watched Crong shaking his dingy beard and crying not to get thrown into the ring. A leper was shaking violently and shuffling slowly down the hall. I suppose it was Crong's opponent. Crong would lose again; the leper had sharper teeth.

Several parties of opponents went by until I saw the cook. The skinny, bearded cook, walked straight down the hall of cages. His stance had a peculiar curve to it, more postured than usual. The strangest thing about his appearance was his huge grin. I hadn't spent much time looking at him before, as it was only glances of him I saw, but the smile didn't suit him. From my bed, I saw only 180 degrees of the world. Everything behind me was gone, and all that was there was the smiling man walking to the cage.

I thought about the forests until I saw him again. It wasn't long before I saw him again. The palm trees and all the tufts of cotton from those cottony trees clouded my mind, and I didn't even think about the blood. The crimson metallic water, dripping down his messianistic beard, his eyes sunken from countless hammerings. I didn't think about the Douglas fir that rooted around his lifeless body, shocked and pumped and slapped and shook all in an attempt to uproot the forest. The flesh that was once made magic with food and ripped its skin from bone with little effort, now turned to bark. On his weathered, beaten old canvas of a face, there hung a bleeding grin.

"Salno, I have your pillow. You asked for it so long ago, and today you earned it. We have one less chef here. And one less occupant." Her third night was no less terrifying than the last. She didn't have the kind of face for her voice. Her face was cold. Tormented, neglected, and so stretched and weathered it was almost old. It was years, that maybe only took a month to occur, that I was seeing.

"Salno, I didn't give you a prompt. I have one for you now. If you can't write about the outside world, write about what happens here. Erin's death is a good start, don't ya think?"

I never noticed before that she held a peculiar shimmer under her sleeve. The robe was long, but just at the bottom of her wrist was a silver line going up her arm. When she sat down on my bed, it protruded, like part of her bone. It confused me.

"A chrome tattoo. It tells the higher-ups that I belong down here. It stretches all the way to my back. I bet you're jealous? It's toxic. The metal makes sure I don't live too long."

"Cut it out then." Why did I care?

"Oh my sweet Salno, it's not possible. It's in the ink." She touched the silver lining, running it up to her elbow, revealing yet more cuts, scars, scrapes, and burns.

"Remove the ink." I reached toward her wrist.

"That's why the tattoo is so long. For someone who doesn't want to live, you sure are in support of my continuing going. You think it's easy for me? Watching that psycho cut up you poor folks, only to toss them back into the ring? We're all trapped here, Salno. We're all going to die here, except you."

"That's unfair." A sweating meth head began banging against the bars, farther down the wing.

"Life is unfair." His neighbor began banging his head against the bars.

"You call this life?" The witch stirred and rammed herself against the bars.

"I call it a legacy. I don't call it life, it's the product of those in favor of population control. Some of us are just meant to die."

"Then why aren't you dead yet?" I asked, hoping to get an answer to some divine question.

"Why aren't you?" was as good an answer as any.

"Because you won't let me. If I could get up, I'd keep trying."

She moved closer to me. Placing her chromed hand against my neck, she caressed the weathered skin. She looked like a mother petting a newborn that would soon be dragged to the holding room, to be rocked into sleep by some crone. "Salno, that's what we need. Such determination for death. None for life. Let that determination be for a good death then." She answered my earlier question.

"What's your name?" Her hand retracted from my neck.

"Somebody else asked me that a long time ago." She almost gasped.

"It's a fairly common question."

"He said it with the same curiosity and ignition that I hear in you. I don't want to be anyone's fire again. Find your own," she stated almost angrily before strutting out of the cell.

I hadn't planned an escape before. I hadn't thought I would ever want to. Here I was, planning. Mr. Green had a big gun, and he thought I was a cripple. I had a strong right hook, and he had rotten teeth. That's simple. I'd like to take Sunflower out with me. Half of me was saying, "Leave the girl, she's only trouble." The other was saying, "There's a reason she came to you. Nobody that wants help says it, that's why you know they need help."

The next day another one died. I still couldn't fight. "Mr. Green, what's the name of the new dead one!" I was able to yell as he dragged them by cart.

"What, laddie? You fancy yourself a newsy then? Fuck off." I just wrote down his description. Skinny and died of a heart attack. Green eyes and dark hair.

When the sunflower returned, I was in a far better mood than the night before. I was in a far better mood than I had been for the past eleven years.

"Have you written anything new tonight?"

"I wrote down the descriptions of the two that died."

"Three," she whispered.

"Three?"

"Jess is looking to him. His name was Michael, coke. He bashed his head against his bunk until it cracked open. Didn't happen but an hour ago." She talked about him as if she knew him.

"Can't hear anything over the howling from here," I joked.

"Yes, it's planned that way. I think they've figured out they can die. The halls will be quieter shortly."

"Four metal transparent walls and toxins sure have a way of rotting away the brain."

"How is it, Salno, that you've spent eleven years watching people waste away and lived without anything to dull the pain." She sat down again on my metal bunk, like the first night she had been here.

"I used to drink. It just made me remember things."

"So you've forgotten things? What's the first thing you forgot?" she pestered, leaning against my battered torso.

"Love," I mumbled.

"Hey, an easy thing to forget. Who made you forget it?" Her head now leaned on my shoulder, forcing me to speak into her ear.

"A girl who made me wait at a dock."

"Ooh, such a juicy-sounding story. Tell it to me please!" she crooned, diving deeper into my personal space, stunned at her proximity to my flea-bitten carcass.

I didn't want to remember. So long ago, when I was stood up the countless times, the many times I awaited her and the many times she didn't look so excited to see me. "Nothing to tell. The harvest never fruited, and so the farmer went home."

"Oh my, so cryptic. There's few things in this world that interest me anymore than a mysterious man named Salno." Her warm breath hid my name from me, as it had been said many times before by many breaths.

"There's nothing that interests me," I said to the groaning other half of the conversation.

"Oh really, the first woman that's shown you comfort in a decade and you have no interest? I know men well enough to know *that's a lie.*" The petals slid down the window, like raindrops. Thousands of petals falling from her mouth to my ears, and I had them closed.

"I wouldn't call this comfort," I said to her explorative hands.

"I could hold a knife to your throat, but I know you'd like it too much, so I suppose this isn't comfort in the sense you're accustomed to. I'd rather not clean blood off your sheets. It's comfort for me, and so I expect it translates mutually." She lightly traced my facial wound with her index finger.

"If all the oceans rose up to fall on my head, held in the palm of your hand, I still wouldn't fuck you."

"I'm offended you thought that was on the table." Her fingernail scraped into the wound as it left my head.

"It's the tone," said my mouth, ignorant of the placement of her hands.

Her lips were now next to my ear, like they had been before. "Well, it was on the table. Not anymore, though." And she left. Not even sure my cock worked anymore.

"Tell me, where are you when you're not on night duty?"

"You'll find it fairly easily, so I needn't give you directions. Tomorrow, you start a revolution, and we lose lots of money. Rest up."

Drowning doesn't hurt like everyone said it would. Drowning in a river, so deep down looking at the car lights forming a chandelier to guide me down. I saw the bottom of a ship, far above me. It looked like a hat, with red and blue stripes on each side. The reds and yellows and blues and all the daggers of refracted light danced above me, following around my rising breath. I was full of water, to the brim like a water balloon. It was getting darker and darker, and the lights stayed with me, now surrounding me on all sides. One of them had lips, and one had a tail, and one had spikes of all shapes. The sea was bottomless. I just kept falling.

The bottom of the sea was rusty, covered in metal rods and pain and blood. Where the blood came from was obvious. It was me. I was bleeding, and so I was cursed to glide over this dark, bitter landscape, suffocating in constant agony until the eels came for me. The eels were not a friendly group. Every time my foot touched ground, glass filled my feet, and so I waded slowly away from the glowing lights heading toward me. The first ghastly creature bore two heads, both purple, and had jagged teeth from each end and red lips. Her teeth ripped into my thigh, the other head gouging open my stomach. The largest eel, a green fanged thing with large fins and a heavily barbed tail chomped into my neck. My blood filled the room. I was now in a room. A cage, a cage that had rusted and bent and broke and if I wasn't in so much suffering, I could have smashed the bars open. So I wasn't allowed to leave. The eels circled my cage.

"You've met with a horrible crux of fate, poor boy," Sunflowers murmured in a watery tone.

Salno, Salno, Salno echoed all around me. Lips of all shapes and sizes and teeth clicking against my eardrums whispering and shouting and bellowing my name. I don't want this. I didn't want this. I never thought this was where I would be stuck. Hundreds of cages, all lined up with mine, different eels of all shapes glued to their faces and breathing in the noxious water they excrete. I cried, I sobbed, and the lips kissed me. They kissed me all over, whispering sweet nothings, unintelligible tones of honey and peppermint. I didn't notice with each kiss, the lips removed my skin, and before it was too late, I was bleeding again, my whole skinless body ripping itself apart. And just like that, I was nothing but bones. The eels took it all. Even my brain, hanging in my skull, was crushed by their gnashing jaws.

"Well then untie them, get them down, and try and wake them, goddamn it! Who knows how long they've been hanging there!" Green's teeth jabbered loudly from a block down the hall. Today I was escaping. I had to. Twenty men hung themselves last night. Perhaps they had the same nightmare as me.

"Where's the little shit that wanted to die? The cripple. Get him out of his cell, Jess, right now!" He stomped his heavy legs against the ground, making the corpses around me quiver. My eyes barely parted to meet Crong's lifeless face, dangled from a polka-dot tie.

Jess had no trouble getting me out of my cell. She had no trouble making me kneel, under the barrel of a gun. The barrel of a very large gun, which would make half of my body paint the cell bars. I had no trouble spitting on Donaldo's disgusting shoes, and he had no trouble reopening the wound in my forehead with those disgusting shoes. He stood on my ribs, one leg bent at an angle where I had a fraction of a chance to perform a foul move indeed.

His testicles were very sensitive, and even barefoot, he fell to the ground. Perhaps it was the addition of pushing him upward and off me, dropping his cocked gun directly onto the ground next to me. It went off, throwing a million particles of fast concrete into the side of my face, and the sound is still missing from me. The silence made for a more dramatic exit.

There were three bullets in the gun, after I shot Donaldo twice. Jess was of no harm to me, having run to some corner of the cages. I didn't care because I was leaving. "Whoever can rip off that man's trench coat, his keys are in it, and all their meds are somewhere out here! I'm no general, figure it out yourselves!" I was speaking to only Jess, as all the lifeless fools couldn't hear me at the moment.

There was no Goliath waiting for me. There was no light at the end of the tunnel. There was a window, just past the cage, past the stands, past the basement, and what I figured was the way out. The stands had an ominous feeling to them, as if the crowd was crying in its own absence. All the fury and vigor from the night, every night, is absent in light. There's a reason some creatures are nocturnal, because they're afraid they'll see themselves.

I found her in front of a window. Several flights of stairs, past the exit doors. I had to find her before I left. She put this ball into motion, and so I couldn't just leave her.

It felt like a romantic scene, her leaning on the railing, in front of a huge bay window. Because of that, I stood next to her. My broken arm twitched, feeling like it should reach out and touch her or feel the nonexistent breeze or something. It was broken, and so it merely twitched.

"Jess isn't going to call anyone, this is a very illegal operation. A surgeon's assistant, you see, so much spilt blood. A surgeon, you spill so much blood. Doctors have a fascination with death, turned on by the fact they can stop it by cutting up bits of people."

"I can't say I agree, Amy."

"Yeah, I know, I'm just spitting out words as usual. They sound nice and passionate and whatever. How do you like the world?" She lit a cigarette, old brand.

"There's too many clouds."

"Oh, that's just smog, dear."

"So that's what happened to it?"

"It's a lot worse down there. Crazy things happen to people these days. The guns are so strong. Certainly got population control out of the way, but damn. However the hell five people could keep all this in check, for so long, I can't hardly believe it. I want to die, and I feel like a god at the same time. It's a shame these windows don't open, I feel like I could fly."

"You probably can't, your lungs are shit."

"Salno, why can you read so fast?"

"Because I haven't had anything worth reading in a decade. I'm no writer."

"Oh, that would explain it."

"What do you think the authorities will say if they find this?"

"Not my business. Do you really want to leave?"

"I'm not really sure."

"It's a good thing you're not in love with me."

"Oh yeah, that would be dreadful."

"There's no time for that sort of thing anymore, the world is too small."

I breathed, and she breathed, and watched the orange smog float over the city below us. There were no trees, no forests, only big building blocks filled with people who all missed the trees. And I was sure the trees missed the people, but they were all drowned.

"I'd offer you a tuna sandwich, but I don't have one," she said, taking a drag very quietly. "I also hung them all."

"I'm really weighing the pros and cons of shooting myself right now, Amy. Gimme a reason not to." I beckon a drag, one I hadn't taken in a long, long time.

"Don't got one champ, you got the ticket, take the ride. You escaped, and what else is there?"

"What a horrible lesson."

"What did you expect? Nothing on the outside of a window ever really looks like it did behind the window." And then there was a flash. A flash to rival all others. The kind of flash from a camera that didn't get clicked by any one person. A collective flash, from a trillion cameras all pointed at the same place and all capturing the visage of all those flashes. The flash bothered them both, but it was distant, and it was what they were waiting for. It was what they came to see.

The flash was what gave them motion. What made them realize others saw this flash, saw what was murderous, what destroyed two cities before and hadn't since. The destruction that would lead to worse, the wars that would ensue. This beautiful cloud, one that would ruin their lives and ruin the world worse than it had already been. Here they flirted with death.

"I thought it would be prettier, honestly," said Sunflowers, a name smoother than Amy to my mind.

TIME OF LIGHTS

Long ago, there were lights at night. Hundreds of years, hundreds of lights. Lights in the night, lights in the day, lights at all times. Every one of these lights was connected by a little string. This string was time. All the lights were souls. Long, long ago, you could see the souls because none of them had bodies yet, and so these lights just floated about like no one's business.

Then one day, a giant monster appeared, so big and strong it could eat the little lights. Once the light was eaten, it could never be seen again for a very long time.

At the same time this monster came, there was a smart light. The light could inhabit the elements around it. One day this soul was floating in and out of elements, and it found something that was working all on its own, without a soul to fill it. The smart little soul had found the oldest creature in the whole world, the large, large tree in the middle.

The soul said to the great tree, "Oh grand tree, I have to do something! All of my friends are being devoured by a horrible monster! Please, old and wise one, tell me what I must do." The tree was silent for a while. Of course it was aware of the monster, but it did not have any reason to fret. It never paid any attention to the souls, because it had a light all its own.

The tree was not cruel, and so it proudly said to the light, "Oh soul that seeks my will, I will grant you a great favor. I will let you inhabit my enormous body. From this, I will gain fruit. When the fruit falls, it will be eaten by insects. Those insects are safe from this great monster. I will let you and all of your friends live inside of those insects and give them a great gift." The soul did not think twice before it agreed to the old tree's offer. Before the tree granted entrance, it asked one thing in return. "When the time comes, you and your friends will not cut me down, and you will not harm the vessels I let you live in." The soul thought a moment. How could an insect cut down a tree so tall and wide? And why would the bugs be harmed? It was an offer the soul couldn't refuse, with no side effects.

Time went on, the smart soul inhabited the tree, and like promised, it gave fruit. Large, delicious fruit, so scrumptious insects of all types crawled to the fruit. The monster howled and cried as it watched its meal channel into the bodies of the insects. Time passed, the fruit continued falling, the insects continued eating, and the souls kept on living. A long time passed on like this, until the insects began changing. It had been so long the souls didn't notice that when one insect died, they were transferred onto its kin. Soon the insects looked different from one another, but bigger and stronger and smarter. The souls learned that they could use these better bodies to eat more than the fruit. Some of these souls banded together and decided they would try and devour the monster that had spurned them so long ago. Then the smart little soul, its soul and body being smaller than all the others, spoke with the great tree again. It told the great tree of what the other souls were planning to do, and the tree did not approve. The tree said, "Though this creature is weak and its meat delectable, this taste is a taste of soul. Any being that eats of its meat will hunt souls."

Hearing this, the little soul tried to run and tell the group of its flaws. Before the little one could get to them, however, the party had already gone hunting. They had found the beast in its lair, and the beast begged and pleaded for its life. The souls looked at its pitiful face and laughed. The creature was struck down mercilessly and carried back to the hunting party's camp, where they roasted it over a fire. As the hunters ate their prize, they grew hungrier and hungrier. Their mouths watered at the taste of this flesh. The party talked and danced after their feast, making plans of another hunt soon to come.

Little did the hunters know that what they believed to be a beast on their next hunt was really an old reclusive soul. This soul was one that liked to keep to itself, living in a cave far away. After killing the creature, they realized their error, but because the souls didn't know this one, they assumed it was okay if they only ate just that soul. So the party ate and danced and sang again, their hunger for souls rising, their refrain weakening.

The little soul heard about their hunger for souls, and fearing this, he ran to the tree again. The tree, like years before, agreed to help the little soul. "I want you to gather up all of the pits from the fruit that you have eaten for centuries. I want you to take them and plant them on the path around the hunters' camp. These will grow into my children and create a wall so tall the hunters will never be able to pass. They will eat one another's wicked souls and will never be seen again."

So the little soul did this, gathering the multitude of seeds and planting them on the pathway. Like the tree said, before the hunters came hunting, the trees created a wall of wood, reaching into the sky. Again, like the tree predicted, they grew hungry. One by one they fought and feasted on one another, until there was only one wicked hunter left. This soul, however, was not tricked by the tainted meat like the others. This soul was aware of its error from the start and merely wanted to eat its comrades. It was dark and evil, and all its light was gone. This soul stayed trapped for a long, long time. The insects continued changing, and the souls continued moving. At this point, the insects appeared almost human. All this time, the wicked soul stayed in the cage of trees, trying to climb out. One day this soul found its way out of the cage by climbing years and years up the trees, weak from starvation.

When this soul reached the ground, it was met with billions of souls all around it. This soul however had grown wise from its exile. It knew that it could not feast until all its enemies were gone. Though it was wicked, with no other soul being seen out of its body, the thing seemed like but another insect walking among humanity.

One day the smart soul was wandering along the forest, now wandering around the trap. When it was walking, it noticed a small thing gesturing to it. This soul was wise but still very naive, and so it picked up the small being. The wicked creature smiled and spoke sweet, soothing words to the bigger soul. It was a great long time that the creature had been traveling with the smart soul. Then the wicked soul saw its opportunity and asked a favor. "Oh friend, how I love traveling with you. I do not know where I would be if it were not for you. I only ask you one thing. Long, long ago, a good friend I had was lost in the roots of that tall tree in the middle of the world. Would you be willing to help me find that friend?"

The soul thought for a moment and decided that as long as there was no harm to the tree that saved them all those years ago, then it would be fine. The wicked snickered in evil joy, hoping it would finally put an end to all its insatiable hunger. Once the travelers were under the great tree, the helpful soul asked where to look for their friend. "Oh, you go on looking that way. I'll stay by the roots and look." The trusting soul wandered around the caves and wondered what kind of friend the little creature was looking for. The soul walked back to where it had left the insect. When it arrived, it was astonished to find the wicked soul had eaten and destroyed all the roots keeping the great tree tethered.

With a final cackle, the creature ran out into the world to begin its feasting. The little soul was so devastated that it was tricked it began bawling under the giving tree. The tree had only given it and its friends kindness. It was so sorry that it betrayed the tree. The tree, now dying, heard the echoing in its roots, and so it spoke. "Do not fret, little one. I have lived since the beginning of time, and I will live on for the rest of it. I would like you, like before, to enter my body for asylum. There you will live on forever. You must try very hard to keep me alive, but from this effort, with every fruit I drop, there will spawn a new soul. That soul will grow, and these souls will replace the ones the wicked one is eating. There will be more good souls than there are wicked, and the world will be happy again, even with wickedness. Your only cost is you will give up life, and you will only see the world from my point of view. All of your friends have forgotten to leave their bodies, I am sorry I had to ask this burden of you, my only age-old ward."

The soul wordlessly passed down to the heart of the tree, granting life to it once more. The next spring, its roots had regrown fruits, and souls fell from the trees, and the wicked one believed it had won. There were enough souls to be eaten, for only the old and weak ones were small enough to be taken by the vile being. This creature began to be called death, for no one ever saw it in its true form, only the aftermath. Eventually every soul would be eaten, but only when it had reached its end. Then the tree, growing taller than ever brought anew. Everything was peaceful in the time of lights.

Rainy Day Hero

The stage lights crashed down upon the leading actress, and her bones were crushed almost entirely save, ironically, for her wishbone. The crew rushed, the audience screamed, and those sick folks like you and I kept watching, to see how her death would affect the performance. She made sure not to utter "Macbeth," but perhaps someone had forgotten to tell her to break a leg. Perhaps whoever put up the lights pushed the wrong button on the light board. The moral of the story is she was dead. The woman who loved her was on the stage, trying to pry her out from under the lights, and I was laughing at it all. Where were you?

You were outside in the snow. Sticking your tongue out as innocently as a woman of your looks can, waiting for a crystal to land on it. You loved that it was finally snowing, that you were alive to see it and you'd be alive for the rest of it. You didn't care that your hair was wet and freezing. You didn't care that the air protested to you being there where you were, breathing so as you were, being existent in this beauty. You didn't go to the performance because you'd seen it the night before. You decided not to go with me, and for your benefit, you avoided paying the thirteen-dollar admission. That thirteen dollars was worth the price of bloodshed, worth the price of laughter and joy and feeling alive in comparison to that poor chicken that got smooshed by the lights. I must sound insane, but believe me, I am.

"You're kidding! Alexandria is fucking dead? That performance *was* her life, she'd wanted to be Lady Macbeth since she was little!" You yelled over the phone.

"It's horribly ironic. It's a bit funny too," I replied.

"A bit funny? A bit, you say? Why the hell are you in police custody then?"

"Because cops don't understand a joke. And I brought bud."

"Jeremy, for Christ's sake, you don't just laugh out loud at a massacre."

"Yeah, I'm well aware. The reason it's funny is because I knew her. Must've been God's will."

"Jeremy, lesbians don't go to hell because they have vaginas and are therefore obligated to go to a shiny happy place in the sky."

"Tell that to her mufflicker. She seems to be in hell right now. She got the bad cop hounding her down."

"That's because cops hate dykes."

"The Christian ones."

I was told another minute and you would have to come pick me up. You didn't. You didn't come get me.

"Okay, Mr. Satchens. Tell me where you were at the scene of the crime." An onion-ring-scented pig said to me. The office I was stuck in smelled like crabs and blue cheese. I'm guessing this guy's wife came by, because he couldn't get a gal that wasn't cheesy sea-food. Whatever appearance comes to mind from that, that's what he looked like.

"It wasn't a crime. The lights fell on her."

"So you were in the audience?" My Mary Jane was in his left hand.

"You handcuffed me, genius." He stuck his hand in and smelled it.

"You were seen committing suspicious behavior in the audi-ence, shortly after her death." He was waving it around as if to prove a point.

"Because I knew her. She was my friend, and this was an ironic death for her, as good a death as any. Of course I was laughing, don't you know how to take a joke?"

"I don't understand what's funny about her death." He took out at least five grams and shoved it in his disgusting gray sweater vest.

"Okay, so the play *Macbeth*. It's cursed, right. You know every time it shows something goes wrong apparently. She was playing Lady Macbeth, a part she's wanted to play since she was little, her mom was a Shakespeare buff, you know? So here she is, right there saying 'All the perfumes of Arabia cannot sweeten this little hand.' Holding it out to the audience and BAM! Lights fall right on her, crushing everything there. That's her final line, and that was her final line. I don't know how you can't see the humor in that."

"So you're saying that coincidentally it hit at the right time, right there. It was a perfect little joke, all for you. The only one laughing." He opened up the damn bag to smell it again.

"Well, if my girlfriend were there, it would have been the two of us laughing."

He took a sip of his coffee. The ceiling fan above us sighed lightly at its own failure to keep the room cool. He stared into me, with those puke-green policing eyes. He didn't say anything for a little while. "Is it illegal to have a morbid sense of humor, Officer?"

I had a lot of time to think about that moment. Sure, this was my dear friend. I loved her and all, but she was a bit of a cunt. I mean, she was full of herself. Practically slit the throats of the other gals that wanted her part. The Clinton ain't the most classy theatre, but it certainly turned up for *Macbeth*. You wanted to audition, but I told you that she'd get up in your face about it. I loved that it snowed the day she died, because it made it seem like it was meant to happen. Like that day was perfect just the way it was, and you'd be happy and I'd be happy and all that shit. I didn't think our apartment would get burned down by her cast members. Thespians are loyal.

So I already spoiled the next bit for you. While I was in the slammer for a month because I had weed on me, our apartment got burned down. Thankfully you were out cheating on me and didn't have a single thing in there that wasn't in your bag. It doesn't matter that I was found innocent, that you were innocent, and you were going to be homeless for a little while, and it doesn't matter to my bastard of a brother that you were living in the snow, because his older brother was an asshole. Kellin, this is the day I figured out that you would divorce me. I learned that I caused you more trouble than I was worth and that you would get tired of it. I want you to know that now because I never told you.

We met at a coffeehouse the next time. The lights were too bright, much brighter than inside the prison. You were wearing green lipstick, that kind you could only get at that gothy store down in Chinatown and those fake lashes that were easy to steal. Who am I kidding, you stole everything you owned. That was one of the reasons I loved you. We were below the law. You more than me, but I'm the one that always took the fall because I never really cared about myself as long as you were happy.

You ordered a mocha, and I ordered a stool and a noose, but they only gave me the stool. "So how's the outside world, gorgeous? It's only been a month, but they didn't give me my bud back, it being illegal and all."

"Did you get raped?" you said in your dark-tinted sunglasses, so I couldn't tell whether you were looking at me or your nails.

"Oh, funny story about that. So the second day I realized I hadn't not banged you every night for like a year, so I was incredibly lonely. So I dropped the soap intentionally, and now in four years I have a boyfriend, when Ramone gets out. He stabbed a man eight times, you didn't stab a man for me." It had been so long since our first date.

"He didn't stab a man for you either." It was in the rain.

"He stabbed a man to MEET me." And you were in polka dot rain boots, and I was in a tank top.

"He didn't know he'd meet you." You kissed me under a bridge, after I pestered you enough about it.

"You have a lot of time to get used to it." Then you said, *Next time we do this, I'm brushing my teeth.*

"Goddamn it, Jeremy, why did you have to go to prison?" I was in the present again, staring out the window past your painted face.

"Because I was gonna smoke out Alex, but then she died." You took off your sunglasses, and I could see your green eyes look different, gone from pond water to the color of jealousy.

You asked Roy if we could stay with him, because I didn't have the heart to beg. Brother like brother, he said yes to you but no to me. So while you cheated on me with him, I worked at the docks and saved and saved and then got robbed by a man named Milo, a queer little fellow who did a lot of acid. I visited every weekend, and you pretended that you weren't cheating on me and so did I because I didn't really care. I suppose that's why you left me. Because you realized I could never care about you or what you did more than I cared about myself or the world, and you realized that I cared about you as little as anything because we take the things that love us the most for granted. I still don't care about you, but at the same time, I do simply because I'm supposed to.

A trip down memory lane like this, I really needed it. What's the next milestone on our genocide of a relationship, Kelly? Is it the day I confronted you, the day I said I hated what you were doing to me and then you proposed, saying it wouldn't ever happen again. The day you found that I'd been homeless because no way somebody my size would get mugged or freeze to death (it was the easiest way to save money) and the day we bought that big ass house with the basement and the rooms for you and me and a daughter and two empty rooms, and the day my brother gave me those two fucking dogs, which I will always hate him for.

The day I want to remember right now is the third, fourth, fifth, somewhere in the series of times you cheated on me. The day I came back from the factory, carrying my old Scooby Doo lunchbox, seeing your clothes strewn about the floor because of our fight last night. The fight about…dishes or something, something so stupid. So stupid that you had to be stupid and brood over it and then bring a man in from god knows where. He was really good-looking, and honestly, Kelly, I wish you'd just talk to me about this sort of thing. I was as much of a freak as you were, but that's why you never trusted me.

So I threw a lamp at him. I really hoped it would break or something, but it just hit his back disappointingly and cracked on the floor. They always say when you find the girl of your dreams, it goes well after that. I couldn't disagree more because you're still the girl of my dreams, and I hate you because of this. Being cucked is pretty damn awful, no matter how promiscuous humans are supposed to be.

Then Roy died. He died abruptly, and I didn't care at all because he gave me two shitty dogs, and I met his son, and you'd been gone for a while. I read that Cain was in a mental hospital, and that shouldn't come as a surprise to you. Your daughter is still in pain somewhere, that daughter that you never will let me meet or let yourself meet, and that awful man whom you said you loved and then ditched him to be with me, then ditched me to be with another man, and god knows who you ditched now.

I wanted Rachel to meet Amy. I talked to you about it, going back into her life, but one daughter was enough for you. You didn't step foot in my house for years, neither did she, because I was bad news. I found a son, and I want you to know I love him more than anything else you could have given me. Just because Rachel has an inkling of genes from you, I can't stand looking at her. Isaac looks like my brother, before he was a spoiled little brat that got everything he wanted, and kept getting everything he wanted and then left Anne on her own whenever he abused whatever he picked up that day. I didn't want to let him end up like that, and I figured I was the lesser of two evils.

So I didn't raise a son. I raised myself, the way our parents didn't. He never found himself going after a girl, except that British bitch, and that's my fault. I told him they're trouble, because every single day I thought about you, thought of a way it could work out, every goddamn day I wanted you to love me no matter how much it hurt me. I am not someone who can fall out of love. I picked a woman, and I stuck with her until the end. I never thought of you as you are now. I always thought of you as that cute little girl with a pixie cut and gorgeous, lucky pond-green eyes who told me she couldn't love. Whom I always tried to hold and she never let me.

I didn't want you to change, and you did anyway. That's the thing about love, the ultimate lesson I learned. Love is projecting, and you stopped being what I loved. I watched my cheeks sag, my soul crumble, my skin wither, and I still saw that pudgy youthful look, and I still saw your hand finally holding mine, finally allowing my love in and letting yourself be weak in front of me, because I was always weak in front of you and always there to help you if you fell.

I want you to know that you are still that to me. I look back, and I miss the you before you loved me. I miss the best friend, the "It's not how you look, it's how you carry yourself." I miss the pining. It's in the chase where my passion was left.

And so I'm looking in the mirror, and I'm looking at myself thirty years ago, and I'm telling him not to chase you, and he's telling me he loves you more than anything in the world, and I'm telling him that I know, I know you love her, but she won't always be who she is. She's going to love you and leech off you, and you'll change her, and she'll change you, and you'll both get sick of each other, and I can't stand another sight of you. I'm a fool. I'm a fool who fell in love and didn't stop before I was too far in. I'm never going to finish this because my computer is broken. I just hit it, and the screen is smashed.

I'm sorry I made you love me, Kelly.

IS IT THAT WAY?

The stranger did not have a horse. She did not have a bag loaded with a hundred niceties. She had a plastic garbage bag and hot-pink medallion eyes. It was a dark day, but not the kind of dark that hurts your temperament, the kind of dark you want after you've had an hour-long migraine and you just want to shrivel up and die. The clouds whispered rain constantly, but no showers were in sight yet.

So she set down her garbage bag, and she leaned against the dead tree in the center of the garden, where all the nothing around could see her, and she took off her boots and emptied the sand out of 'em. She did it a silly way, making sure to unlace each boot and carefully remove them before tipping out the sand. Seemed a bit roundabout, but what really is roundabout these days?

The crisp leaves under the bag crunched as she rifled through it, tossing out tools and blankets and hats and stuffed animals until she found herself a pipe and put it in her mouth. When she inhaled, it was like the tree behind her faded, and all the turmoil and danger she'd faced to get here was over, and she could just relax. I suppose that's the purpose of herb in the afterlife, to feel calm amidst the horrors.

Her eyes got glossy and red but just matched the pink of 'em, and so it looked fitting. Born stoned, gone through life like it, I suppose. She's a stranger. You can't know nothing about strangers but what you make up, because they're strange, and so you don't talk to them. It's that fear that they may not be the good folk you want them to be or the fear that you won't be a good enough folk to them. More so the latter these days, ain't nobody got loyalty these days, except the ones that hide in the shadows, those ones see all and fix all. I'm one of those.

She had herself a bracelet on, looked like it was beaded with teeth. She tossed her hair around, let it flow in the subtle breeze, and sighed to the open air. The house that used to be on the edge of the field had food in it, and I wished I could tell her that, but it was against policy. It's the few rules we have; that's why we're inferior, and everything else runs about. That's why we're the last of human kindness, and they're our hostels.

She fell asleep when nightfall came. O'Brien told me that she had no business on our grounds, that she must go in the morning, leave her a gift and a parting note. Send her an omen, he said. I couldn't write a good omen these days, so I sent her a jar of honey. A jar of honey should be enough for her to keep alive. It was a shame I didn't have any roots around.

We put the torches up around her so the prowlers didn't get her. The prairie was safer than others in the terms of man, but not in beast. We learned to calm 'em with the right light, and so it was what we did. A candle that burned just a sliver above darkness, only enough to calm a beast. They lay there, around the camp all night, even perhaps docile enough to pet, but don't you dare. Their snorts and sniffles filled the night, and the pink-eyed girl slept on through all of it, completely unaware of the trouble she was in.

I noticed something peculiar about her in the early morning light. A group of crows followed her. Ain't seen crows since death left the prairie, and they had nothing to eat. How did I suppose she kept them things fed?

The garden ain't much but a few onions and a lot of strawberries. None of them in bloomed well enough to be eaten, but enough that if you were starving, you could rip 'em up. O'Brien always asked me why I kept on tending 'em, couldn't eat anything anyhow. I say, we may as well be a good host when somebody like this showed up.

Something's supposed to keep the world alive, since the live one's ain't doing it.

She got up a bit after dawn. She saw the dismembered hand on the stick that we put up next to the tree, in it resting the jar of honey. It was real funny getting it set up, because O'Brien wanted to be able to connect all the tendons to a puppet-wand-type deal, but he couldn't get 'em taught enough, and it just felt all awkward to mess with. I hate messing with the sleepers, but we needed a message that would go through, and she got through.

O'Brien said I should follow her, said that if I kept an eye on her, it might help her chances of survival. How long we been waiting around this prairie for a journeyer? He wouldn't go with me, but I knew I didn't need him. He needed to take care of the fort.

She didn't have a weapon, which I didn't understand. Even I carried around my fishing bat, for when I found something bigger than a man. How she gotten to here, out hundreds of miles from any humans, I couldn't understand. She was walking out toward the old crumbling church, in the corner up west of here. I thought a few times about running ahead of her and checking it out, make sure the little lady didn't get hurt, but then I questioned what part of me was saying that, and was it a part of me that was decaying? So I didn't. I just looked how she clumsily placed her footing, unaware of the moles and the worms and the ant lions that were under her feet. No matter how close she stepped to danger, sometimes tripping over it, she was unscathed. This was a being of luck.

She stepped cautiously through the arch, her eyes fixed on the crucifix in the center of the room. The visage of Christ long stolen; only the rusty metal cross remained. She said something to it, something about *all the help she hasn't gotten and all the hope she spent getting here.* No graveyard, no lake, no orphanage where her sister was waiting for her. I looked over at a crumbling pile of gravestones, and a quote stuck out to me. "Life's a big joke. Nobody else down here right now figured that out."

I questioned how long she spent to get here, thinking her family was what she'd find. I got no answer. I only breathed the words. She heard them none. I thought that perhaps if I let my presence be known, then I could somehow help. I could stop her from crying. I could stop her from feeling so terrible. It was my first journeyer, first one I'd seen ever since the fall. I wanted to help her so damn bad. I hadn't thought much about the meaning of families and the meaning of having somebody caring for ya. When the ol' thumper quits a thumpin', you forget impertinent things like that.

So I did what I thought wouldn't jeopardize my position, which was sit down outside the church, letting my bare, cold feet scrape against the dusty ground. I heard a sharp breath and a brick crack against the wall of the church, and I jumped up to hide myself, but she was upon me 'fore I could. Her calloused, warm hand gripping my neck like a chicken to the slaughter. "Deadfella, what business have you with God?" she hissed into my ear. In the other hand she held a shard of brick, aimed between my eyes. I couldn't think for a moment, unsure of what to say.

"Deliverin' a lost soul, I suppose" was all I could utter. It was all I could think that had to do with the present situation, my lost soul being delivered to whatever's after, or hers being delivered to where it belonged. I couldn't really hear what she said after that. A slur of insults, threats or pleads, prayers, I couldn't tell anymore because I was watching her crows. I saw those red dead eyes in the bigger one, the one standing atop the church, where the old bell used to hang before O'Brien cut her down to build a strange sort of tech thing. I don't remember what it did, because it didn't work anyhow. It was in those red eyes that squawked of hunger and that black clicking tongue. I realized what she fed them crows just as the brick smashed my temple and I fell.

I was fishing, on the shores up north. I was in my worker's boots, dippin' 'em in the water 'cause Pa wasn't there to tell me no, thinking that I'd get me a bite on the toe. That wasn't the case. I just watched my feet float up whenever my legs got tired of pushing the weight of those boots down. Reminds me of that poor sleeper, the one with the bricks on his feet in that same lake. He had himself a fancy white suit, long dyed by algae and silt, and his hands had all but been bitten off completely. But I wasn't looking at that poor gambling man right now. Right now I was catching the biggest, bluest catfish I ever would, before all the catfish got eaten up and I couldn't fish no more. I was still a hungering, still breathing, still urging. Still desiring. Still desiring that neighbor girl, the one who tended to the henhouses and I always got to see her bend over to lay the feed, and we both knew I was watching her, and she made extra time by cleaning out the feed boxes once she caught on to my peepin'. Those were times, those were the days I like to think about. I can't remember her name for the life of me, hold the joke, and I can't remember how far away she lived. I can't remember nothing but me catching that catfish, and her supposed to come over and see the fish and trade it for a kiss. I think that's how it went. I suppose when you're long dead, you start mixing things up, making 'em more romantic than they really were. But that didn't happen after I caught the cat. This time, those pink medallion eyes came walking down the pier, smiling like I didn't know her tricks. She dropped that ol' bag and said, "What a catch that is," and I say, "Splendid thing." And she said she knew something good she could give me for it and reached into that bag, and she was still glaring those pearly whites at me, still keeping that glittery, unnatural eye contact until I saw that brick out the corner of my eye and dropped the cat to duck, and it was too late. There I was, sinking into those old, deep waters, wearing a fancy white suit and trying to gasp for air. I couldn't gasp because my lungs were filled with water, but I knew they weren't really filled with water. It was just my stomach and my brain telling my throat to close up and hold tight, and I couldn't float on up because of the cinder blocks on my feet. I was screaming at her, but she couldn't hear me because she was not here anymore. Nothing was here anymore. It was just me and the deep dark abyss that was coming into me.

I hadn't slept in longer than I could recollect, and of course the first dream was a damned nightmare. I looked up at the church wall behind me, and the barred door next to where I was laying. I could hear the dusk approaching. I could hear the rooting. That snorting coming from miles away. I could hear her pacing behind the wall, still freaking herself out with thoughts of family and life and safety. I did what I could to get up, noticed I landed funny on my left hand, and now I broke more fingers, and now it couldn't be used until I bothered to fix it. The church was on a hill, and from that hill I saw them. Prowling for anything that was alive or dead, anything they could stick in their mouths what has blood in 'em.

She was walking back and forth on the dusty ground, tip-tapping, not knowing what her noises were attracting, let alone her words. "Okay, Delphine, get a hold of yourself, get a hold of…Jesus Christ what if I never find him, what if I never find the grave, what if I get eaten by that zombie or his friends or the moles or anything out in this bumfuck nowhere town! Why is it me, why did I have to go find him, why am I in charge of finding the godfather? I love him, as much as ever, but—"

"Open up, ya dumb bitch!" I hollered, banging my arm against the door as hard as I could. It ain't like the movies. You don't get inhuman strength, ya don't get a hunger for blood, ya don't become a vegetable only capable of murder, if this narrative ain't made that clear, and ya don't infect nobody. Some'f us die, and some'f us don't. I don't decide it, and she don't decide it. God don't decide it. It just happens.

I could hear her hitch. She thought she'd killed me, I figured so anyway, and then I heard her begin to cry again. I kept knocking, a bit softer now, a bit slower, as the moon came on up and the tusks began banging on everything that looked like it needed to be rammed. I coughed, coughed up whatever you might call vomit, choked out whatever my putrid voice box might call a cry and begged. "You don't understand, you can't understand, you need to get out of this building! We're on the same side here, neither of us wants to be pig shit, and your blood-flowing prejudice should be able to understand that!"

She only screamed harder, and I couldn't take it no more. So I did what I thought I could, picked up the bloody rock and smashed at the rotted wood door. The whole building wouldn't stand up, let alone her or this damn door. I curled the rock round my fist and smashed it hard as I could, ignoring the pain and the hurt and the cries of repulsion from the dame inside. Why was I risking my neck for this ungrateful woman anyway? I gave her honey, and that was the hardest thing to find this side of nowhere, so I may as well make sure it ended up in her belly and not shattered on the ground like a jar of old grease.

I remember it was by the time I heard thunder that I knocked that door open. There she stood, holding out a crucifix as if I were a Dracula or something, eyes pouring like a fountain and hands jittering harder than a jet turbine. "Listen here, there's bigger problems than a zombie for you to deal with, I don't plan on eating you. Those boars, they do. They'll be here in less than five minutes, and we have a mile to go until I get to my candles. You know that tree you slept on last night? We're running to it, you can follow me if you want, but either way I'll be taking back that honey." And I snagged it right out of her bag and ran out the door.

It's hard to rely on the human adrenal gland for endurance when you don't have a functioning adrenal gland, so I just pretended I had one. I jogged on down that hill, tripping on my big toe and crashing down, bruising myself up more on the scratchin' dirt. I heard it, lying on my belly, feeling deader than I ever have. Fear of death is nothing. What I fear is living. I fear that my brain will keep on going after those big fuckers crunch it all up and digest it, and there I'll go on thinking, lying in a pile on a prairie, only to be trampled the next day by the same boar that shat me out. That's why we fear the prowlers, because we seen what they do. Took us a hundred tries to find out what made em calm, took a hundred un-lifes to fight this silent war.

I heard that thunder, smelled that rancid smell they had. Like a hundred landfills, put into a garbage compactor and set on fire then soaked in a water closet. I closed my eyes and put my one hand over my face, hoping I didn't see the end, but I couldn't help peeking. All I could see, through my pinky and ringer, was the old church. That door hanging open. Then a crash, a scream, and bricks began falling down the hill. *I'm still alive, I'm still capable,* I told myself, trying to rouse the strength to push myself up. It wasn't until those pink medallion eyes were watering on down the hill, sprinting toward me, that I knew I couldn't give up the goose now. Ain't nobody been able to outrun a boar in more than a few feet of it, and this little lady did. I knew that I told her I wanted that jar, and since I was using it as an excuse to keep her alive, I might as well find it. I found it, smashed against my stomach, bits of glass stuck in everywhere I could see there wasn't honey. Now they could smell me, now they could tell I was not just a corpse they could pick at later. Now they knew I was game. And there was the Beast.

The warty old steamboat-sized mammoth of a pig, chasing on down that hill after the stranger, after that worried sister that we all knew. His brown clumpy trotters hitting the ground like jack-hammers, crushing down the dusty earth flatter than it already was. His shiny, blood-stained battering rams were what knocked the bell tower down. They knocked the food house down. They knocked down the institution. Those tusks knocked down the whole city of Cornelius and everything in it except me, O'Brien, and the gambler. He left the gambler for his peers.

My feet moved on and on down that stretch, the stranger running way ahead of me on account of her newer limbs. The beast was personally hunting us. His cronies were circling around us on all sides, the stench unbearable and the sight hideous. Fungus grew under their fur, mold in their eyes and mouths, bloody maws from biting their own tongues in hunger. The smaller ones were hungrier because the beast always ate first.

The tree was in sight, O'Brien's green eyes shining at us in the darkness. He already lit the candles, and I could feel the proximity of the beast. Gaining speed now that he was on flat ground, gaining ground on pride and hunger. Then I recalled something. I recalled that the beast didn't quell from the candles, that he was the exception and that was how he got so damn big. He ate all night, normally ignoring the camp because we ain't worth it. But tonight I was worth it because I was covered in life and running after life.

So I did what I figured I'd end up doing anyhow, sacrificing myself for a woman with pretty eyes and getting my chance at it. At the Beast. At the king of pigs, the king of liars, and there I was, the thief of the dead, the poor country boy who just wouldn't stay in the ground. Here I'm going to feed my princess the royal jelly. It's silly how something like a little romantic thought like that, a little passion, can stir such energy in an old body like mine. My fucked-up arm relaxed, swinging to the beat of my sprinting legs, needing no air and taking no time to stop. I gained four hundred feet on the beast, causing him to roar and rip up the ground with his tusks. Flung-up dust clouded my eyes, covered 'em totally, but I knew where I was going. The only place with weapons, the only place with food, and the only place I didn't dare go.

The foundation tingled as I stepped rotting foot on it, awaiting me. The cellar door was locked, and I still had the key around my neck like I said I'd keep in case he ever got himself stuck down there. In case his boy went with 'em, met with the devil and signed his body over for eternal motion. And there he sat, in the chair he was sitting in when he screamed how I was lying and how Satan tricks us using the ones we love most. I can't blame him. He died happy thinking I'd meet him up in that big shining fishing hole in the sky. I would've used the key, but I couldn't see my Pa like I was. I just wanted to.

It took me a minute to remember where he kept everything, rifling through the drawers and cabinets and then remembering he kept the guns in the refrigerator, because a zombie'd think he was in there for a snack and blow their brains out. That was where I found the elephant gun, and that was where I found the lance. Only two weapons I would need to kill this thing.

I'm not going to tell you I shot him in the head from long distance, straight through the brain and on ways to the heart, knocking him dead and curing his crew back into cute little piglets. No, siree, I got gored. I stood my ground, holding out that lance, having the gun wrapped round my back by parachute cord, looking him dead in the eye by a hundred feet. At seventy-five feet I could see his pupils, meeting mine, knowing my plan and not caring because this was a battle between two kings. This wasn't a pig and a fisher boy; this was the dead fella with a gun and the pig with a body count. My rotting heels ground into the ground, left and right held over my head aimed toward the head of the beast, that was how I got stabbed through the gut, dropping the spear before I could even scrape him, tossed into the air, given a few seconds to look through my gut down at the beast, and grabbed again by his teeth. He stole my calf, and I watched his black oily tongue scrape my flesh from it like a prime rib. Dead flesh was chewier, and I thought he just realized I was not dead, because now I was pulling out my gun and pointing it at the charging thing. All I could do was take that one shot. Take it, take it, take it, wait, wait. The boar stopped. He was looking down the barrel, seeing through me and seeing through me. My dead, cold eyes met his blackish yellow globes, and he saw I wouldn't give up no matter what he ripped off me, and his front hoof hit his back hoof in a mighty trip. His tree trunks kneeled down, crashing to the ground. His tusks imbedded in the ground, and I saw something leave his eyes. He's died of something else. If I hadn't known better, I wouldn't have pulled the trigger. I never known whether or not he was really dead or not, but I know that murdering gray bastard don't have a brain no more, and that his goddamn tusk is my new leg.

That's what I'd like to say. I'd like to say that I hobbled back on over to the tree, that I sewed myself up some beautiful clothing to cover up my hole. That I went on tending my garden, and we defeated the pigs, and the afterlife was hunky dory again. It never was. This was just my time, the gambler had his time, O'Brien will have his time, and my pa had his time. I don't know how long I been laying here, but I ain't been eaten yet. Maybe she made it, maybe she didn't. All I know is I ended a great thing that day, that I ended a beast, and I did it without a life, and so any of you fucks that think it ain't worth nothing should better untie the rope.

Sometime, the last words I heard in a while, I heard a conversation. I felt something come out of me.

"Damn shame, good gardener he was. Now he's sleeping again. Damn good thing he did, killing that beast."

"Where'd he get this jar?"

"Oh, I gave it to him. Some fella in Portland gave it to—"

"What, you just looked at me funny."

"You want the simple one or the long one?"

"Portland? That's twenty miles away, and it's full of deadfellas like you."

"Not completely, if our old peer is still kicking around. Have a good journey, Delphine, you're not here tomorrow, honey."

OUT, OUT, WITH THE WINDOWS IN THE ATTIC

I haven't seen my brother this morning. He's still sick in the attic, and Mom says we can't go inside because he'll give us the measles. I haven't seen him in a week, maybe two. I kind of miss his face. Not because of its shape or nothing, it just belongs here, two of the same face. It's a paired face, my face. I don't like my face being sick.

Mama is out gardening in the rain. He's up there looking down at her because that's what I've always seen him doing up there. All winter. It's been more than a few weeks. Mama is whistling on about it like she didn't know what he wants from her. He wants a hug. I can't give it to him either. I want to bring him his bear or his hats or maybe some of my toys for him 'cause Mama don't buy him none. But I can't slip him anything under the door. If Mama sees me sticking things under the door, she'll pick me up and carry me downstairs, but sometimes I can slip him a note.

The attic is a funny place. It's over our upstairs kitchen through the dropout staircase up above us. You pull them stairs down, and you walk on up, and there's a door in front of you. You're in the attic hallway, and it's locked. It's been locked all winter because Cain has the measles.

Dad's over the pond, they say. That's what everybody that comes in to talk to Mama says to me. Getting those dang gooks out of Korea, they say. Bombing them up and down the race track, they say. Then they go into the patio with Mama, and she says to go pick up some milk. The men are always different, and they never come back again. I wonder if Mama ties 'em up and locks 'em in the attic, and that's why she hasn't let him out in a long time.

Twice a day, she brings him a meal. It's never the same meal she cooks for me. She says for her special boy she makes us a supper for two and then gives Cain cereal or fish heads or sometimes old spaghetti. I always wondered what fish heads taste like, but she never makes 'em for me. Maybe I won't ever know, since he can't come downstairs and tell me. I wonder when winter will be over.

Cain asks me if I can go tell Kelly he loves her. I tell him that I can't talk to Kelly. Mama says so 'cause she's a mean girl. I ain't never seen her be mean, but I know that she's probably right since she always sees everything when I'm not looking. She tells me Kelly throws eggs at the windows up there, and I don't know what Cain could love about having eggs thrown at his windows.

Kelly ain't very big. She's a bit taller than Cain, and she's got pearly red hair. Cain tells me pearls are not red, and I say no but their tongues are, and pearls come out of their tongues. He says not to say his girlfriend has clam-tongue hair and not to say "ain't" because it makes us sound uneducated. He asked me yesterday when winter would be over, and I said maybe a few more months. We're having a long one.

She hangs up some garlic paintings in my room, says Jesus likes garlic, so nobody'll come and steal my blood. I ask her why garlic is scary to blood-thiefers, why just a li'l onion makes 'em all queasy. She says not to worry about it none, and that when she sees one, she'll kill it before it can even get close to my room. She hangs a big scary cross in the living room, with a big bloody statue on it. I don't know why Jesus has to be dead up there, why he has to be bleeding all gory like all over our floor, why do that scare 'em away? She says they don't dare touch the blood o' Christ, that it'll burn 'em right up.

Kelly comes by this morning, not for any real reason, but she's asking where Cain is. I say he's up in the attic until winter ends. She looks puzzled when I say that, and I say "What?"

"It's summer, Terrence." I tell her not to call me Terrence. Terrence is Papa's name. Call me Terry and I won't get upset please.

She looks up at them attic windows, and I see my brother's smiling face looking down at her clam-tongue hair and mouthing words to her. I ask her why she likes my brother so much anyhow. "He's smart, and he don't do everything his mama says. I sure as heck know boys gotta get their measles shot when they turn ten. Prolly before they turn ten." I told her the blood-thiefers like to hide in vaccines and so Mama won't let us get 'em. She wants to keep us safe.

She just looks back up at the windows and frown. I can see brother put his hand up to the glass, hoping somehow she'd fly on up there. I don't like her much. I tell Mama what she says about him, that it isn't winter and she doesn't think he has measles anymore. She says, "What does that little tramp know about seasons and my son." I say, "I don't know, Ma, I don't know anything about it." She asks if I've been talking to her, if I believed her crazy little stories. I tell her, "No, Ma, I really don't, I believe whatever you say. I'm my dad's son, and he's my brother, but he's not my dad's son."

Mama doesn't keep any pictures of dad up anymore. She used to when he just left for the war, but she's certain he's run off with some Korean floozy. I don't know what a floozy is, but when they shipped his uniform back in the mail with a pretty flag on top, she threw it on the ground. She screamed about how it's a lie, how all this S-word was a lie, and Satan was just putting her on and that man of hers ran off with some Korean floozy. That was her exact words. I got it too. Me and Cain both do that, 'member everything we hear for good. Can repeat it back like a parrot if I try hard enough, but Cain does it better than I do on account of his bigger brain. But I got cleaner blood'n him, so it's even.

She used to read a lot, my Mama. She has a hundred dusty books, and when Cain was first beginning to read, she used to let him borrow them, and they'd read together. Then he started remembering them better'n her, and she started to think he was tryin' to trick her. Mama knows she knows everything. Even though she sometimes makes mistakes, I make sure she knows she knows everything. Cain don't.

Mama always painted that blood on Christ ever since we got the thing. Muttering to herself about something or other, occasionally making a prayer and crossing herself and going back to painting it on. She's a sad ol' woman. Sometimes she cries while doing it, begging Christ to protect her boy and fix the other.

Dr. Doe comes over this morning, saying he's heard my brother has the measles. He says it's real late in the season for the measles and that it might be something more serious. He says his daughter was worried, which made him worried. He asks if he could speak with Mama. Mama comes on down the attic stairs, carrying her red bucket to paint the statue, but when she sees the sliver of light in the doorway, she walks right on up with that bucket and leaves it in the hallway. I know this 'cause I counted the steps to the attic hallway and hear 'em going up or down.

"Ma'am, Little Terry here was telling me you have a sick boy with the measles. I—"

"He's all better now, Doctor, just been waiting a few more days to see if he's feeling better is all!" she calls down. That's what she said to him the last time Cain got sick too. Cain gets sick a lot. She's washing her hands in the kitchen, red running off them from the paint. She's muttering something about a spot, and she can't get the paint off.

"Ma'am, for the sake of my daughter, I'd really like to check on your son. They're such good friends, you know, and—" I can hear that Cain told him to say that. I can hear Cain mouthing the words upstairs, any trick to escape.

Mama comes on out with a wooden cross in her hand and puts it in the doctor's hand, the one he has leaning on the doorway, that's over my head. I wonder what it would be like to have a doctor as a daddy. This is when Mama comes over to him, her baggy green eyes looking him straight and mouthing strongly, "All he needs is prayer, Doctor, the boy is fine." I can feel Cain putting his hand on the window and shaking his head like he does when all his tricks are up. Mama tells me to leave a stool by the door so I can look out the peeper, and if it's the doctor not to open it.

The birds are singing today, and I think it's not winter no more, and so I tell my mama I miss Cain real bad and ask if he can come out. She says he's still too sick, and he still has to make her paint so he can heal. That's all he does all night is make that red paint. Jesus is red now, can't even see the shape of his scrawny arms, and all the paint drips on down to the carpet. I'm carrying a meal on up to Cain when I remember it's our birthday.

"Hey, Cain, happy birthday! Hey, Cain, I bet I can open this little envelope thingy here if I get a hammer, I wanna give you some of my cake!"

I couldn't get no sleep last night because I was listening. I was listening to Mama's night singing, the night singing she does to keep 'em away. The blood-thiefers don't like her voice. I found a hammer and got the little shoot open. I don't think Mama knows where it is since it's all the way at the bottom of the door. She don't look down. I never figured why.

Papa wanted to be a sailor, but the government wouldn't let him. I suppose that's why I think about sailing sometimes, think about not sailing sometimes. It's always sailing, whether it's the absence of sailing or the presence of sailing. "Fucking prick!" my mama screams into the phone, while I'm looking at my knots book.

I hear a dropping of something heavy upstairs. It isn't until I hear his wail that I realize it's Cain. I never gave him the hammer. I just opened the shoot. She's throwing him now, throwing him against the walls of the room. I can't focus on the toe-knot or the horse-ran-gle or any of those knots I need to know because all I can hear is his screaming. All I can hear is the blowing of the breeze through my empty head, and I can't tell what I'm hearing. I don't know what drove me to it, but I walk on up, thump thump thumping my feet up those stairs, quieted by the louder thumping of Cain, thumping away his heart and thumping away his body.

"The reason he ran away with that Korean! I knew he was doing more than dropping bombs, you infectious boy. I knew he caught something, CAUGHT ONE OF THOSE LITTLE DEVILS AND PUT IT IN MY WOMB, THERE TO STRANGLE MY BABY! It's because of you that Terrence is going to grow up broken. You don't deserve that hellish mind of yours, Cain! He can hardly read well enough as think, and here you are reading Shakespeare at ten! You think I wanted to marry a freak and have a worse one? You think I wanted to potty train one son for half his life and have the other one correcting me? It's bad enough having a retard, and I have a genius too. You're disgusting, Cain!" Every time she says another sentence, she throws him against another wall, holding him by his wrists, his measles cuts were dripping all over the walls.

It's hard seeing my brother like that, seeing him all purple and broken and beaten down for all he's doing is being my brother. She doesn't see I'm watching. All he has ever done is wear my face, with a few smarter words coming out of it. Dr. Doe comes in right about then, right about when she throws Cain down the stairs, and I stand at the top of them, looking down at his dying blue eyes, full of tears and hurt and blood and brains. He was ol' King Duncan, and here was his death, and I only know that 'cause Mama used to read us that play, back when we was little and couldn't read ourselves yet. She always hated how that king had so many friends and all Macbeth wanted was a happy family. All he wanted was a wife that loved him and didn't strangle him in the womb like my brother done to me. There lay my mama's bloody hand, sighing in exhaustion, glaring down at my dying brother and dripping her motherly tears on my hair. Doctor came in with a few officers, and that's when me and my brother moved to Portland.

That's really all I can remember after that, because all I want to do now is sail away from my mama and sail away from my brother and sail away from those blood-thiefers that infected him and infected whatever he births. I just wanted to be clean. The attic windows broke when I saw that house again, because Cain broke 'em with that big red bloody face of Christ.

Everything about the Music Box and Why I Stole It

Well, James, if you ever learn how to read, then this is dedicated to you. My absentminded little tyke, looking up at me from your muddy stroller, having watched all the shit I carried you through and never speaking a peep about it. I hope to god that you learn to read. If nothing else, you learn how to read what I put down on this paper, breathing harsh and painful and all over the place to the beat of that fool man's piano. I never ask you a thing else, is all that you learn how to read. I know you ain't a bright kid, I saw it when you came out of me, but I know that you will be able to read.

Before the war, I dreamed about having a kid. I never would have discovered some higher power if I didn't have you, poor ol' simpleton in a harsh, complicated world. Needs somebody that ain't me to watch over him, and that's why I'm telling myself this whole lie. But I know if I keep on lying to myself, I'll eventually believe it and die on believing. My father wasn't religious, and his wasn't religious, and neither is your father, wherever he is, but my mother was, and my grandmother was, and I suppose I may as well be too.

The desert wasn't a place for a woman, I knew that for sure. I knew the minute me and Ike landed here that ain't no place to raise a family and no place to keep a woman. But I suppose that's because I wasn't a woman then. I was a little girl hoping to see what was left of the world. Ike saw this opportunity to make us some money and

166

a cold lonely place to play his harmonica at night. No matter how hard he tries to play for me, he never sounds as good as he does when he thinks I'm not listening. Or he did, until the fall came. You keep hearing everybody say things about that or I'm sure you will. I'm not sure you'll even survive. But the fall was a war.

We don't call it World War III for a reason. We call it the fall, because we fell. The human race fell because of it. Too much industry. The war was started over the oil supply. Not enough petroleum left in the ground for the common man to make it to work in the morning, let alone fly a banana to a grocery store. All the powers were hoarding what they could. Saving it for the planes they'd use to bomb the rest of the world. In times of disparity, man tries to conquer. Man tries to climb his way to the top, without realizing what it is they're climbing on top of. I can't hold them accountable. It's in their nature. It's in your father's nature. That might be what he's doing right now, trying to climb on top of the table, hoping somewhere in the ceiling he'll find bread to put on it.

The scientists all talked about nuclear winter, talked about ways that nukes would destroy the world. It wasn't like that at all. We didn't understand that something that came from the ground worked well with the ground, that just because it's glowy and shiny and we can use it to crunch and munch the world all up, it was something man had power over. We didn't hold uranium in our hand; uranium held us by the whole body. First it was the States that dropped bombs on everybody. Dropped 'em on Siberia, dropped 'em on Korea, dropped 'em on England. And that took up their petroleum. With our big buildings and our fancy cars and our dark, isolated lives. Then, the rest of it came. The isolated little walled-up country got their bubble broken.

I can't describe to you the horror they were left in after the nukes came. They obliterate everything, they do, except for nature. With an abundance of radiation, the world took different shape there. It took different shape where the rest fell. It got into the air, it got into the water, it got everywhere, and thankfully, the ones who had enough money had prepared for the total obliteration and fixed up their homes, and the smart ones like me and your father and Amy and that merry little band of fighters she'd picked up and the creep and the doctor and the minx with the pink medallion eyes, we all fled down to Mexico. We all had loose ties with them. We didn't know each other. We had a few things in common. Amy is your second cousin. She's dead now, don't you worry, but it's all these loose ties what kept us alive. The radiation made some live, zombies, the undead, ghouls, whatever you'd call them, we owe a good debt to them too.

Luke couldn't die, neither could his wife, neither could the doctor because they're something else. The only three pupils of the Friar left alive, and left alive by technicality. Born of the earth, from the earth, and ain't shy to radiation. Here these scientists are, not judging the properties of minor radiation like they judge major radiation, not realizing how it affects time, linearity, lifespan, personality, etcetera. Radiation ain't just something we learned to fiddle with. It's something that's been here. Something that the Friar figured out eons and eons ago, and all he wanted was to live a bit longer, 1,700 hundred bits ago. He knew how it'd all play out, and well, he brought on a few of his students, the one he wanted to save, *the one he thought was worth saving*, and the one who thought she'd learned too late.

We ended up in Brazil, where my real father was from. This was right after America dropped the nukes, and so we walked all the way down the border, split off a few times, but we knew where we were going and how to get there. You weren't even a glimmer in my eye yet, and your father wasn't even sure he wanted to be in love yet. His uncle had some business with marriage he didn't like, and him and his uncle were very close. Your grandfather died young, far too young, and so did your great uncle. Your great uncle would have loved you. He wouldn't care that you were simple. He'd throw you up in the air and say "Less brain just means more room for giggling!" and blow into your belly. That's how he was toward the end of his life. He was a jolly man, less full of crude humor and more full of just utter joy. Ike will plead to you he wasn't a happy man, but I saw him, I saw the way he looked at Ike and the way he looked at me and the way he would say to him, "So you landed a rich bitch, huh? Just like me. Well, don't let her sell ya off to the black market." And he'd look over at me, and he'd smile through that squirrely brown beard he had, and I would see he wanted to shed a tear. Jeremy was that kind of man. When he wanted to cry, he'd only shed a tear and then tell a bunch of jokes. Jeremy committed suicide shortly before we were engaged. Jeremy never knew we were in love. Isaac had the audacity to rent out a hooker to dance with him on Jeremy's grave. That's a story too. It's in Isaac's journal. I'm sure you'll read it when you find him…If you find him.

Luke and Delphine, I didn't know them very well. I knew Isaac's shrink, who moved here in twenty-five on account of her now learning to be a proper psychiatrist. Said some fella named the Friar told her to come to Portland and sew up the blanket he started. She didn't know what that meant, but in the grocery she met me and asked for my husband. I told her, "What do you know of my husband for?" She said, "I know his name is Isaac and that he needs some serious therapy." She ended up staying in our home, and her associates stayed in the basement. Delphine had strange eyes, pink ones. She's dead now too, out somewhere in old Hillsboro looking for Luke. He's running from her because she doesn't know why he's running. Running for killing the only person she loved, the Friar. At least he thinks she loved him, but Julian tells me the news with everybody. She's only following him because she's his milk and honey, and what's tea without that?

When something's powerful, there's always a catch. Delphine's was envy. Luke's, his was fury. All the immunity and pain tolerance to resist and handle any kind of impact but twice the fury from any impact in place of the pain. Talking about the impact of not being told the world's going to end and that he'd have to live through it, well, that was too much for poor Luke. That was enough for him to bash in the brains of the poor old turkey. I never knew him, but apparently he didn't deserve that end.

That's when we found the music box. Well, not really exactly when we found it. We heard of it. From two bozos on the road to Mexico, can't get their languid hands off each other, telling us about some sort of box playing the sweetest tune it could cause a boar to lay down, a sleeper to wake, a deadfella to remember something, and a hallucination to become reality. That's what they said, and they talked about it, and they walked with us for a while as we went on back to the States. Why'd we go back to the States, you may be thinking, after all we'd done to get to safety? Because Ike wanted to put some flowers on Jeremy's grave. There wasn't no grave. Delphine found that out. Her sister and Jeremy shared a cemetery. We never got there. We never even got over the border. Some phony border inspectors up the road from it acted like they had business to stop us. Hannah was shot, the shooter said something about her glowing, but the shooter was hopped up on steam. Anti-radiation drug slows your cancer but hurts your brain. That was when I saw the box fall out of her pocket. That was when I saw Ike see me see the box, and that was when I grabbed it and ran off down south again, baby in my belly and Isaac holding back Art. Art was a big guy, a very big guy, and Isaac wasn't the strongest. He just had a way with words. They both did. They could match wits for hours on the road, and when they were enemies, they matched wits harder.

See, Art was trying to track me down. I tried the box when I got to the right place, but no sort of regular music box key could work with it. Required some special sort of key, one that Art had. Isaac was smarter than Art, but Artemis was paranoid and crazy. Burned down the places he thought I was, knowing that the metal box would be left unharmed. He didn't know which one was the one, 'cause Hannah never let him near the damn thing, so he kept them all in a bag he carried over his shoulder everywhere he went, house to burned-down house, looking for his bride's box. Isaac chased him down, chased him into a corner, passed misinformation to him, and locked him in one of his own fires in El Salvador. Around this time, Julian was helping me with the baby, you, who'd been born back in Brazil in your grandfather's old house. Julian was a clairvoyant. She chose what the Friar chose, knowledge and life. She told me what your father was doing, to the minute detail. I can only summarize his journey like this because I'm not sure you'll understand any big words. He went about everywhere on this side of the globe, not just because he had a purpose, but because he needed a purpose.

Isaac, he had the key now. He found it in Art's shirt pocket and thanked him in his dying breath for reuniting him with the love of his life. I know the box made 'em crazy, because it was making me crazy. It contained the lost voice of every little dying soul that ever had the pride enough to hope. It's been making me crazy. I can't half see what I'm writing anymore. It changed my dialect. You never would've believed me If I told you I used to speak in the primmest, propperest English.

Luke, what did he do? He got lost. He got lost in his head, in his desire to die. He hated the Friar for the gift, having to watch everyone in the world die while he was left here with a few survivors. He didn't seem to have much love for humanity, but when it was gone, he sure did. He got separated from me and Julian after Delphine needed to find her sister. We were staying in a little home in the mountains, trying to raise you proper. Sometimes she'd look at you in a way that I knew meant she knew something I didn't, and it was something I didn't want to know, and so I never asked.

He went west. He went up to Portland, where the Friar first met him. I never met the man, because he never came with us. Julian sort of took his place as their leader, but he was never really a leader either. She told me he couldn't see anything past the fall, that nuclear power only had so much of a view. You can see far, far into the future, but it always ends at some point. I never asked her how far she could see now, and I never wanted to ask. It ended at the fall for him. So he walked around the crumbled metropolis, aimlessly waiting for his end. He didn't know Luke was on his way to put an end to what the Friar started, but he figured that if he waited around long enough, one of his remaining pupils would show up. It was Luke, and he had a pipe, and he had his hands, and that was the end of it. It's strange, how the king is so easy to kill when you're down to three pieces and one of them changes color at the last minute you're pretty screwed. I hope you learn to play chess. I hope chess is still around then.

It was around this time when we met Amy. She had a car. That's how we knew her, because she had a car. You were six months old, still couldn't hold your head up when other kids would be babbling. You stayed silent, and so did we. She wanted to kill you when she met you. Said that we were banding up a crew to go start a life again. She said the boys needed drugs, and they needed someone to cook them. Her right hand stopped her from putting that bullet in your brain. Salno, the saint he was, he told her every life was worth it. He asked her where she first met him and what she had done for him and how his bandaged, bloodied body was any more valuable than your burbling baby body. He was able to convince her that because most retards have incredible strength, he'd be useful when he grew up. We didn't take into account that she was an aging woman and that she wouldn't survive much longer. Just on account of the way she'd been living. She chose substance and crime, and so I suppose that's how our family always is. I'm the purebred, and your father's the rabies-ridden mutt that came from wild dogs. Ain't blood related, you two, just the daughter of a man named Cain, who had a fling with Jeremy's wife, and bam. The poor girl was dead from the start. Dad was a loon, and his fool brother was too. Julian left something out about her, and I'm real glad she did, but I know it had something to do with her shiny tattoo.

We did learn something funny about Amy, though. Our mate Delphine killed her first love. He became a crossdressing fag, and we only knew that because he was one of Julian's patients. I heard the story before, but I didn't think about it from that angle. How could someone like Amy have seen anything in him? Never met the fella, I can't tell ya.

I learned to make meth on the road. I learned to make crack. I learned to make heroin. I learned to make cocaine. I learned to make everything but the drugs that don't kill ya. Lost a few men my first few tries. I got all right at it, and that's where we spent your first year. In a small encampment down by the Gulf of Mexico, right on the green ocean, making fixes. Inky green, the kind of green you see on ivy. That's the radiation. Fish are a lot bigger now than they used to be.

Isaac ended up coming on back around that time. That's the only time you saw your father, and I remember the day. There he came in, pilot's jacket on bloody rags, Brown hair half singed off, wearing a hundred stories I couldn't hear yet in his pockets, limping into the camp. Amy took care of him, patched him up from his journey, damn good surgeon she was she said he wouldn't make it. He had a twisted knee and a hole in his arm all the way through. The only thing he said to me was "Hey, darling, what've I missed?" And then dropped the little brass key into my hand and fell face-first on the dusty ground.

I twisted it up while your father was being patched up. It was a three-hour process. It would've taken longer if I hadn't turned on that box. Every turn I took, I felt a tingle, a harder tingle, a wave of energy shot into me when I let go of the key, and the softest song played. It was harmonic, light and quick, going from low to high with a duet under it, but between the notes you felt something more. You felt the cries, the emotions, the leftovers of our emotions that floated away when we died, and all of 'em were singing at the top of their lungs with that little box. I can't say that I saw the lights. You don't see the lights. You really don't. Just your eyes seeing a wave of light and telling your brain what you think it looks like, but really you're just seeing what your eyes see. That'll make more sense when you play the box when you're older. Brilliant lights of green and purple and blue and hundreds of other colors that light can't make, half of them being sounds, a fourth being tastes, and all of them still the same as lights. I saw them all, all of them fly into my Isaac, kiss all over his broken, beaten, dying body. Sing you to sleep away from your crying. Light all the torches so we saw the boars, tell Amy to look at her mirror, something she said she'd never do again twenty years ago, something that told Luke he should turn around and smell the road behind him. The music box is faded and dirty now, but back then it read on the back a simple title in typewritten ink: "Love Story."

See, pigs like the radiation. It makes them grow, while it kills us or makes some of us rise up again. It's a strange thing. Those pigs, they like to crush us out since we spent all our existence beating them down. They saw an opportunity to take top dog, and that was the fall. About thirty-five of them charged our camp, and because I played that music box, we saw them a mile away. Amy had guns, they had weapons, we had an electric fence, and yet we still lost. Took out at least twenty of them, but the rest were big, bigger than five of the ones we could handle, and they shredded our party to bits. Julian, me, and you, we took off. We stole the truck that ran on piss and vinegar, and we left. It's a cowardly thing to do, but we knew. I knew I had to get you out of there. Before we drove off, Julian looked back at the camp, told me that Isaac would survive, and only Isaac would survive. It was because they thought he was already dead, and he'd wake up with a concussion from being thrown by the beast. I knew Amy and Salno would be happy with that. They saved one last life before losing theirs.

The car stopped before we got anywhere. We got ten miles away, if that, We could still hear the clopping thunder of those pigs, charging on south on their rounds. They go from coast to coast. Every half year they keep a charging.

The box started talking to me, telling me where to go and what to do. I didn't dare play it, but when I left the key in, it played itself. The tune always played in the back of my head, because I stole the box and so the box was flattered. It wanted me to hear it; it needed me to understand this language of lights. Julian left me a few days ago, said the box was poisoning me, and she wouldn't let it. She wouldn't watch it. She left to find her peers, knowing as much as they desired to they wouldn't be able to die so easily.

I can hear them now, James, whispering to me what they want me to do, what they say I have to do, and that's why I'm writing this. That's why I need you to read. I need you to pick up this letter when you're old enough. The song on the piano just ended, and that old guy is going to come tell me it's time to close up the bar. Few of the bars left in Arizona. Ironically, one of the few places that ain't cancerous to live in. I'm sure you'll like growing up here.

The box tells me I need to kill you, James. I'm not going to do that. I'm going to leave the box with you and hope it raises you right, learns not to hate you. Learns that just because your improbable existence fucked it all up that I won't let my only son die. That I don't care if the human race is just a big made-up story now, or that all we have to do is sit down and wait and the air will kill us faster, because I knew how it was before. I could love. Life was simple. All the people I knew were people once, that we all sat on this happy little globe and kissed and hugged and cried and painted, and could get upset about a simple frown or a little sigh and think it matters, in comparison to all this.

I guess I'm being too dramatic. You'll be fine.

PROLOGUE

The sun set on an empty night in the city. I looked around for all that I could see, but everything was dead. I'd not known it, not known it well at all even when I lived in it, alive and bustling, as Lucas tells me it was. I clutch James in my arms, smiling at the sunset, as if I hadn't seen one in a while.

"There's something in your eye," Isaac says.

"Why wouldn't there be, it's a dark day."

Strangely enough, O'Brien ran the ceremony. An awful tradition, one that only mortals performed, and not Isaac nor I, with what he'd gone through, could call ourselves that. The one who had the most memories of the lines ran it. O'Brien looked at me and smiled a strange smile.

"Why so happy on this day? I'm not happy. The love of my life is in that box, and you're not even sad about it!" I scream at the deteriorating flesh before me. I realize how selfish it is and how ironic.

"At least he didn't get back up, D," said the dreary companion. Isaac was speechless, and I set James down, to toddle and wobble around the walkway.

So I did what I felt was right, ignoring cemetery rites. I opened the box and looked at the face that once disturbed me, that once filled me with envy. Envy of his strength, of his ability to keep going despite darkness clouding his eyes. Half of him was missing, and his face was missing. We all end up like this, someday, maybe in more pieces. I could only call it a shell, but a shell he would've liked disposed of properly.

"I'm in disbelief. How'd he croak?" I hear Isaac say to O'Brien, not able to let a curious notion fly away.

"Beekeeping. They eat meat these days…Well, he'd do anything for his honey. Forgot to put on the keeper's net one day, and he was dinner." The dead casually talked to each other like gamblers at a card table.

A cattail popped when I dumped him on the waterfront. Where he wanted it thrown so it'd wash up one day and give some poor kid a good scare, but no kids left to scare, and no flow to take him away, so he sunk in the pond at the deepest point in the Willamette. Then, the cattail popped, and every single one of its seeds hit me in the goddamn face. I could've heard him mumble a nasty joke, or maybe it was just old deadfellas chattering their rusty maws.

ABOUT THE AUTHOR

Nathan Nakonieczny is twenty years old and lives in Hillsboro with his aunt Barbara Nakonieczny. The cottage they share with many cats and a few fish, lizards, and snakes. Nathan has been writing all his life, but this is the first novella he has produced.

CPSIA information can be obtained
at www.ICGtesting.com
Printed in the USA
BVHW082127280223
659395BV00002B/151

9 781647 012984